Glasgow Directories

John Tait's Directory for the City of Glasgow

also for the towns of Paisley, Greenock, Port-Glasgow, and Kilmarnock,

from the 15th May, 1783, to the 15th May 1784, etc

Glasgow Directories

John Tait's Directory for the City of Glasgow
also for the towns of Paisley, Greenock, Port-Glasgow, and Kilmarnock, from the 15th May, 1783, to the 15th May 1784, etc

ISBN/EAN: 9783337409159

Printed in Europe, USA, Canada, Australia, Japan

Cover: Foto ©Andreas Hilbeck / pixelio.de

More available books at **www.hansebooks.com**

JOHN TAIT's

DIRECTORY,

FOR THE

City of Glafgow, Villages of Anderfton, Calton, and Gorbals; alfo for the Towns of Paifley, Greenock, Port-Glafgow, and Kilmarnock,

FROM

The 15th May 1783, to the 15th May 1784.

CONTAINING.

ALPHABETICAL LISTS of the Names and Places of Abode of the Gentlemen, Clergy, Merchants, Traders, Mechanics; and all other Perfons in public Bufinefs; where, at one View, you have a plain Direction, pointing out the Streets, Wynds, Lanes, Clofes, and other Places of their Refidence in thefe Towns.

TOGETHER WITH.

Separate Lifts of the MAGISTRATES, Minifters, Procurators, Phyficians and Surgeons, Midwives, and Meffengers at Arms, alfo the arrival and departure of the Poft at and from Glafgow. Carriers quarters, Stage Coaches, &c. &c. &c.

GLASGOW:

Printed for JOHN TAIT Stationer, the Publifher, and fold at his Shop a little above the Crofs, by the Poft Mafter, and Bookfellers of Paifley, the Bookfellers of Greenock, Port-Glafgow, and Kilmarnock. MDCCLXXXIII.

DEDICATION.

A LIST of the MAGISTRATES and Town Council of the City of Glafgow.

Patrick Colquhoun, Efq; Lord Provoft, merchant Argyle Street.

Alex. Brown, Efq; merchant Bailie, Horn's court ditto.

John Riddel, Efq; jun. ditto Shortridge land ditto.

John M'Auflan Trades Bailie, feeds merchant Argyle ftreet.

James M'Grigor, Efq; Dean of Guild, merchant Candlerigs.

George Buchanan, Efq; Treafurer, Brewer Argyle ftreet.

Robert Auchinclofs, Efq; Deacon Conveener, Cooper Trongate.

Alex. M'Call, merchant Millers ftreet.

Richard Marfhall, wine merchant Madeira court.

Walter Neilfon, merchant Candleriggs.

John Douglafs, merchant Millers ftreet.

Robert Dunmore, merchant ditto.

John Coats Campbell, merchant Virginia ftreet.

William Coats, merchant, head of Gallowgate.

Robert Findlay, merchant, Millers ftreet.

Gilbert Hamilton, merchant, Queens ftreet.

Henry Ritchie, merchant, Adams court.

Jofeph Scott, merchant, Queens ftreet.

Alexander Low, merchant, Adams court.

George Milne, jeweller, Trongate.

William Craig, timber merchant, Clyde ftreet.

Walter Lang, baker, Trongate.

John Miller of Weftertown, Millers ftreet.

James Brodie, fadler, Gallowgate.

John Robertfon, wright, Argyle ftreet.

James Muirhead, fadler, Trongate.

Robert Arthur, taylor, Currie's clofs high ftreet.
Robert Smith, wright, Candlerigs.
John Morrifon, wright, Argyle ftreet.

Reverend Minifters of the Gofpel.

William Craig, D. D. St Andrews parifh, head of Candlerigs.

John Gillies, D. D. fouth or College church parifh, Dunlop ftreet.

William Porteus, weft or wynd parifh, Dunlop ftreet.

Robert Balfour, eaft or outer high church parifh, Charlotte ftreet.

William Taylor, D. D. north or high church parifh, high ftreet.

John M'Caul, fouth weftor laigh church parifh, Trongate.

William Taylor, St Enochs parifh.

Archibald Bonnar, north weft or Ramfhorn parifh.

John Burns, Barony parifh, high ftreet.

William Anderfon, Gorbals, kirk ftreet.

John M'Leod, free presbyterian meeting-houfe, Bridgegate.

James Steven, ditto. ditto. high ftreet.

George Henderfon, burgher meeting, fhuttle ftreet.

Alex. Perrie ditto. Charlotte ftreet.

John Jamifon, antiburgher meeting, Anderfton.

James Ramfay, ditto. Claythorn.

Thomas Bell, relief meeting houfe, ditto.

Falconer, Englifh chapel, Trongate.

Robert Lothian, entry to St Andrews church.

Profeffors in the Univerfity.

William Leechman, D. D. principal, high ftreet.
Robert Findlay, D. D. divinity, new court.

J. Clow Logick, new court.
George Jardin, affiftant, Colledge Court.
John Young, greek, ditto. ditto.
William Richardfon, humanity, new court.
John Anderfon, natural philofophy, ditto.
William Hamilton, anatomy and botany, high
　ftreet.
Alex. Wilfon, aftronomy, new court.
John Miller, civil law, ditto.
Patrick Cumming, oriental languages, ditto.
James Williamfon, mathematicks, ditto.
Hugh M'Leod, church hiftory, ditto.
Thomas Reid, D. D. moral philofophy, ditto.
Archibald Arthur, ditto. Colledge court.
Alex. Stevenfon, M. D. medicine, high ftreet.

Faculty of Procurators.

John Marfhall, fheriff fubftitute, Salt market,
John Findlay, park houfe.
John Wilfon, one of the city clerks, gallowgate.
Robert Barclay,
James Ritchie, Queens ftreet.
James Clark, high ftreet.
Thomas Grahame, head of Stockwell Trongate.
Claud Marfhall, laigh kirk clofe.
John Maxwell, fenior, Moodies wynd.
George Thomfon, Trongate.
Archibald Givan, oppofite poft office, Gibfons
　wynd.
John Snodgrefs.
John Robb, Trongate.
George Riddoch, Salt market.
George Smith, ditto.
Robert Crofs.
Jofeph Crombie, Donalds land Trongate.
James Buchanan, Saracens head inn.

Matthew Gilmour, high ſtreet.
John Maxwell, junior, Horns court Argyle ſtreet.
James Oſwald, Kirkintilloch.
JamesGrahame, Trongate.
John Wilſon, junior, Salt market foot
Robert Græme, Salt market.
Robert M'Aullay, Trades land.
Robert Park, gallowgate.
John Hamilton, Salt market.
Archibald Grahame, Thiſtle bank.
Benjamin Barton, Buchanans land Trongate.
John Scales, head of new wynd ditto.
James M'Lehoſe, London.
James Cunniſon, Jerristown.
David Scott, Salt market foot.
Alexander M'Culloch, Gallowgate.
John Dillon, Salt market.
Archibald Smith, ditto.
John Lang, new wynd.
David Hutchiſon, Salt market.
John Sheils, entry to St Andrews church.
James Mathie, Salt market.
George Crawford, head of Kings ſtreet.
George Muir, high ſtreet.
John M'Ewan, laigh kirk cloſs.
James M'Nayr, Kings ſtreet.
John Leckie, Trongate.
Alexander Robertſon, Argyle ſtreet.
William M'Aullay, Trades land.
Robert Grahame, Trongate.
Archibald Simpſon, Caſtlepens land high ſtreet.
John Purdon, Gallowgate.
William Lindſay, laigh kirk cloſs.
Thomas Falconer, laigh kirk cloſs

Officers of Excise.

Stewart Alexander, Collector of Excise King's ſtreet.
Johnſton George, ſuperviſor of ditto, Dowhill.
Ogilvy Gilbert, ditto. of ditto.
Bane Donald, officer of Excife, Salt market,
Briſbane Robert, ditto. Adam's court.
Bruce John, ditto. Candlerigs.
Corbet Peter, ditto. Bridgegate.
Coggan Hugh, ſenior, ditto. high ſtreet.
Coggan Hugh, junior, ditto. ditto.
Coggan Alexander, ditto. ditto.
Dempſter John, ditto. Calton.
Gibſon John, ditto. Salt market.
Hogg Selby, ditto. Jamaica ſtreet.
Harris Robert, ditto. Anderſtoun.
Jackſon James, ditto. Gibſons wynd.
Johnſton James, ditto King's ſtreet.
M'Donald Angus, ditto. Jamaica ſtreet.
M'Farlane James, ditto. Grahameſtoun.
M'Farlane John, ditto. King's ſtreet.
Moriſon James, ditto. Gallowgate.
Oſwald Henry, ditto. ditto.
Porteous George, ditto. Jamaica ſtreet.
Rutherford John, ditto. Shuttle ſtreet.
Rowand Andrew, ditto. Jamaica ſtreet.
Rowand Archibald, ditto. Argyle ſtreet.
Semple Robert, ditto. Gorbals.
Steedman John, ditto. Anderſton.

Physicians.

Alexander Stevenſon, M. D. College high ſtreet
Peter Wright, M. D. Trongate.
Robert Marſhal, M. D. Argyle ſtreet.

Robert Wallace, furgeon, king ftreet.
Hill and Monteith, Trongate.
Alexander Dunlop, Argyle ftreet.
Charles Wilfon, Stockwell.
William White, high ftreet.
Mr Simpfon, king ftreet.
John Jamifon, ditto.
James Parlane, Stockwell.
Andrew Morris, Dunlop Street.
Archibald Young, Trongate.
Archibald Stirling, Salt market.
George Cochrane, King's ftreet.
John Cree, high ftreet.

Midwives.

Mrs Campbell, high ftreet.
Mrs Cochran, ditto.
Mrs Henderfon, Gallowgate bridge.
Mrs Hewat, head of Maxwells ftreet.
Mrs Hunter, Gilmors land high ftreet,
Mrs Merry, Dowhill.
Mrs M'Rechten, Maxwells ftreet,
Mrs Miller, high ftreet.
Mrs Parkhill, Dowhill.
Mrs Park, Saltmarket.

Meffengers at Arms.

Archibald M'Adam, Salt market.
John M'Adam, ditto.
James Park, ditto.
James M'Farlane, ditto.
George Anderfon, ditto.
John Fergufon, Gallowgate.
John Murdoch, ditto.
George Purden, ditto.
Daniel M'Aulay, Tods land high ftreet.
Robert Wylie, Trongate.
Archibald M'Arthur, Grammar fchool wynd.

JOHN TAIT's

DIRECTORY

For the City of GLASGOW, &c.

From May 1783, to May 1784.

A

ALlans Wilsons and Co. merchants high street.
Allan Richard, of Badowie, ditto.
Allan Richard, junior, merchant, Jamaica street.
Allan, Blackie and Co. merchants Bell's wynd.
Alston John, senior, merchant Argyl's street.
Alston John, junior, ditto. Trongate.
Alston James and Co. silk mercers, Trongate.
Aiken Turnbull and Co. merchants.
Armour Robert, merchant, Trades land Salt market.
Allan Barr and Co. merchants, high street.
Allan Coats and Co. yarn merchants, high street.
Anderson Jonathan, merchant, high street
Anderson George, merchant, Argyle street.
Auchinclofs John, and Co. merchants, Gallow-gate
Auchinclofs William, merchant, beyond Gallow-gate toll.
Austen John and Co. lawn and cambric manufacturers, Bell's wynd.
Archibald Robert, manufacturer Gorbals.

Arthur Thomas, lawn and cambric manufacturer, high ſtreet.

Anderſon James, manfaƈturer high ſtreet.

Adam John, manufaƈturer, Trongate.

Allan James, woolen and linen draper near Croſs Gallowgate.

Adam Andrew, hoſier, high ſtreet.

Aiken William, hoſier, old Vennel.

Anderſon David, woolen and linen draper Gallowgate.

Anderſon and Imrie, haberdaſhers, Argyle ſtreet.

Aiken John, woolen and linen draper Gallowgate.

Allan William, ditto. Trongate.

Anderſon John, ditto. high ſtreet.

Alexander John, teller, Thiſtlebank, Gorbals.

Armſtrong William, accomptant in merchant bank, Argyle ſtreet.

Aird James, toy and muſick ſhop, King ſtreet.

Anderſon John, hardwareman, Trongate.

Aitchiſon Walter, dealer in foreign and britiſh ſpirits, Gallowgate.

Anderſon Thomas, dealer in foreign ſpirits Stockwell.

Angus James, grocer and tea dealer, Trongate.

Auld Peter, grocer and ſpirit dealer Stockwell.

Arthur William, grocer and ſpirit dealer, Trongate.

Angus Mrs, grocer and ſpirit dealer high ſtreet.

Anderſon James, ditto. Bridgegate.

Alliſon Archibald, Auƈtioneer, Salt market.

Aiken Robert and Son, taylors, Gibſons wynd

Arthur Robert, taylor, high ſtreet.

Anderſon Matthew, taylor, Candleriggs,

Anderſon John, taylor, king ſtreet.

Auld John, wholeſale tobaconiſt, high ſtreet.

Alexander John, tobaconiſt ditto.
Anderſon William, ditto. ditto.
Anderſon James, wright, Gallowgate.
Anderſon John, ditto. Barrowfield bridge.
Allan William, wright, beyond old toll Gallow-
    gate.
Alliſon James, ditto. Bridgegate.
Adam John, maſon and architect, Adam's court.
Anderſon John, bricklayer, beyond old toll Gal-
    lowgate.
Anderſon James, baker, high ſtreet.
Anderſon James and William, manufacturers,
    Virginia ſtreet.
Anderſon John, tanner and fleſher, old vennel.
Aiken John, maltman, Havanna ſtreet.
Aiken James, brewer, Gorbals.
Anderſon Adam, copper and white iron ſmith,
    Bridgegate.
Adam John, hammerman, new vennel.
Adam Alexander, printer, Gibſons wynd
Anderſon John, Grahame ſquare.
Alexander Matthew, comb-maker, Gallowgate.
Adam Mrs, tallow chandler and ſoap maker,
    Trongate.
Arthur James, innkeeper, high ſtreet.
Aiken John, ſtabler, ditto.
Alexander Robert, barber, Gallowgate:
Auld William, Greenock carrier, ditto.
Allan Alexander, gardner, Queen's ſtreet.
Alexander John, teacher of dancing, Argyle ſtreet
Allan John, fleſher, king ſtreet.
Allan John lint-heckler, old vennel.

B

BELL Peter, merchant Gallowgate,
Barns John, merchant, Horn's land Argyle
ſtreet.
Barbour Robert, north ſugar houſe, Candleriggs.
Blackburn Andrew, merchant old vennel.
Bogle and Hamilton, merchants and inſurance
brokers, Exchange Trongate.
Blackburn Peter, collector of the ſtamp duties,
Stockwell.
Bogle Robert of Shettleſtown, Queens ſtreet.
Bogle John, merchant, Adam's court.
Bog le Scott and Co. upholſterers, Trongate.
Bogle and Jack, woolen drapers, Exchange.
Bogle Michael, timber merchant, Queen's ſtreet.
Bogle and Scott, ditto. Clyde ſtreet.
Buchanan and Co. merchants, high ſtreet.
Brown Carrick and Co. wholeſale linen printers,
Bell's wynd.
Brown James, merchant, Gallowgate.
Brown George, merchant, Stockwell.
Bogle George, brewer and victualer, Candleriggs.
Bowman John, merchant, Virginia ſtreet,
Brown James, merchant, Jamaica ſtreet.
Briſbane Robert, merchant, Adam's court.
Brown Lowrie and Co. merchants, Trongate.
Brown John, maſter of works, King's ſtreet.
Blackwell Robert, merchant Salt market.
Buchanan Robert, merchant, Jamaica ſtreet.
Bnchanan George, merchant, ditto.
Buchanan Andrew, merchant, ditto.
Buchanan William and John, Sun fire inſurance
office, ditto.

Buchanan John, merchant, Curries clofs high ftreet.

Buchanan John, of Auchentofhen, Trongate.

Bogle Archibald, upholftery warehoufe, ditto.

Brownlee James, merchant, St Enochs burn.

Bailie and Inglis, haberdafhers, Trongate.

Baird Andrew, woolen and linen drapier, high ftreet.

Barr and Ronald, glovers and hofiers, Trongate.

Brown William, glove-fhop, ditto.

Begg Adam, woolen and linen draper, ditto.

Buchanan James, woolen and linen drapier high ftreet.

Buchanan and Leckie, ftocking fhop, Trongate.

Burnfide John, merchant, Salt market.

Bell Mifs, harberdafher, crofs high ftreet.

Baxter Daniel, bookfeller, Salt market.

Bryce John, Printer and bookfeller, ditto.

Bell Peter, pocket book maker, Trongate.

Bell William, printer Gibfon's land.

Brown John, pocket book maker Gibfon's wynd.

Buchanan Alex. bookfeller, high ftreet.

Bryce James, ditto. bridgegate.

Brown James, fpirit proof maker, Trongate.

Bell Walter, grocer and fpirit dealer, Salt market.

Buchanan Thomas, ditto. high ftreet.

Blair Robert, ditto. Gallowgate.

Borland Hugh, grocer and fpirit dealer, bridge-gate.

Bruce Thomas, ditto. high ftreet.

Buchanan Thomas, ditto· ditto.

Buchanan Archibald, ditto. Gallowgate.

Buchanan Mrs, vintner, Saracens head inn.

Buchanan Mrs, vintner, Salt market,

Boyle William, grocer, Gibfon's wynd.

C

Buchanan and Duncan, grocers and ſpirit dealers, high ſtreet.

Bryce Patrick, ſpirit dealer, high ſtreet.

Barclay John, vintner, Salt market.

Barclay John, ditto. high ſtreet.

BeveridgeHenry, ditto Trongate.

Brebner Alex. vintner, Currie's clofs high ſtreet.

Buchanan John, ditto. Trongate.

Buchanan John, ditto. Argyle ſtreet.

Buchanan William, ditto. burnt barns.

Bald Peter, dry falter, Salt market.

Buchanan Bernard, ditto. high ſtreet.

Black David, tobacconiſt, Gallowgate.

Birral Robert, ditto. ditto.

Boyle Mr, ditto. king ſtreet.

Brown James, yarn merchant, high ſtreet.

Buchanan Andrew, ditto. ditto.

Barr John, manufacturer, bun's wynd.

Barr Matthew, ditto. ditto.

Blackwood John, ditto. new wynd.

Brock James, ditto. bell's wynd.

Buchanan John, lawn and cambric manufacturer, Calton.

Burnſide William, manufacturer, high ſtreet.

Brydſon Thomas and Co. jewellers, Trongate.

Bogle Clark and Co. coach makers, Gallowgate.

Brown Daniel, watch and clock maker, high ſtreet.

Borland James, oil and colour man, Trongate.

Brown James and Co. ditto. and painters, ditto.

Buchanan Thomas, hatt maker, Trades land.

Buchanan John, ditto. Trongate.

Blair Miſs, boarding ſchool, Trades land.

Blair Mrs, linen drapier, crofs.

Balmanno John, druggiſt, Trongate.

Brown William and Co. feeds and nurſery men Trongate.

Brodie James, fadler, Gallowgate.
Buchanan William, ditto. high ftreet.
Ballantyne John, copper and white iron fmith, Gallowgate.
Bell William, iron monger, ditto.
Baillie Alex. engraver, Trongate.
Begbie John, carver, bridgegate.
Barrie James, land furveyor, Gallowgate.
Barr James, late rector of the grammar fchool, high ftreet.
Braidfoot John, one of the mafters of grammar fchool, ditto.
Burns John, teacher of Englifh, ditto.
Bower Mr. preacher of the gofpel Shettleftown high ftreet.
Burnfide Thomas, fugar boiler, Gallowgate.
Balderfton William, baker, high ftreet.
Berrie John, ditto. Salt market.
Blair George, ditto. Gallowgate.
Brafh John, ditto. high ftreet.
Brafh John, ditto. Gallowgate.
Brown John, ditto. high ftreet.
Brown Peter, ditto ditto. ditto.
Buchanan William, ditto. ditto.
Buchanan Mrs. ftay maker, Argyle ftreet.
Buchanan John, ditto. Salt market.
Buchanan Alexander, taylor, Gibfon's wynd.
Baird James, ditto. high ftreet.
Bandochie Alex. ditto. high ftreet.
Blair George, ditto Gallowgate.
Blair Daniel, ditto. high ftreet.
Boyd Thomas, ditto. Trongate.
Bogle Matthew, ditto. Bridgegate.
Brackenridge John, ditto. high ftreet.
Broadley Archibald, ditto. ditto.
Brown John, ditto. ditto.
Boaz Mrs. Stay maker, Gallowgate.

Barker George, cordner, Bridgegate.
Barton Henry, ditto. Trongate.
Bryce James, ſhoe ſhop, King's ſtreet.
Brown David, ſhoe ſhop, Gibſon's wynd.
Bryce Andrew, cordner, Dowhill.
Brown James, ditto. blackfriars wynd.
Brown James, ditto. new wynd.
Brown Thomas, ditto. ditto.
Burns James, leather cutter, high ſtreet.
Burns George, ditto. Gallowgate.
Brownlee Archibald, cordner, Salt market.
Buchanan Andrew, ditto. Gallowgate.
Buchanan James, ditto. Trongate.
Boyd William, ditto. Salt market.
Beugo Gavin, tanner, Lancefield.
Buchanan George, ditto. ſpout mouth.
Buchanan William, ditto. Salt market.
Braidſute John, toyman, ditto,
Blyth Colin, founder, ditto.
Buchanan John, Hammerman, Stockwell.
Baxter David, miln wright, broom o'law.
Bennie John, ditto. Grahame's ſquare.
Barclay John, wright, Virginia ſtreet.
Buchanan Archibald, ditto. blackfriar's wynd.
Buchan David, ditto. Argyle ſtreet.
Buchanan Archibald, at Mr Craig's wood yard.
Burton Thomas, glew maker, bridgegate.
Brown Robert, barber, Argyle ſtreet.
Brown James, ditto. Gallowgate.
Brakenridge Thomas, ditto. Stockwell.
Barr James, hoſier, Maxwell's ſtreet.
Black John, ditto. Gallowgate.
Black Alex. ditto. wynd head.
Black Matthew, ditto. Gallowgate.
Brown Archibald, ditto. King's ſtreet.
Brown John, ditto. ditto.

Betham James, hofier, Gallowgate toll.
Buchanan William, ditto. ditto.
Begg John, teller, merchant bank, Trongate.
Boyd Andrew, accountant, Thiftle bank Maxwell's ftreet.
Bachop John, porter, Glafgow arms bank.
Bell William, at Mr Houfton's Argyle ftreet.
Baillie John, accountant, bell's wynd.
Black George, baillie of the N. W. and college church yards, Salt market.
Bogle Mrs. keeps callender, Bell's wynd.
Bogle Robert, book binder, Salt market.
Boag Andrew, china and ftone ware dealer, Trongate.
Bowie Archibald, brufh maker, Gallowgate.
Balcanquhal and Henderfon, cork cutters Trongate.
Baird William, mafon, fpout mouth.
Balloch William, farmer, buckie burn.
Bell William, carter, candleriggs.
Banantine Alex. junior, Inn-keeper, Trongate.
Barr Robert, grocer, Salt market.
Bell Robert, grocer and fpirit dealer, Gallowgate.
Bruce Thomas, ditto. high ftreet.
Black James, apothecary, foot of old wynd.
Blair Archibald, japaner, Gallowgate.
Bogle John, cotton dealer, ditto.
Bryce William, gardner, Queen's ftreet.
Brown John, dyer, Argyle ftreet.
Brown and Stephen, yarn merchants, high ftreet.
Bowes John, maltman, calton.
Bruce Robert, bellman, King's ftreet.
Buchanan, George, ditto. high ftreet.

C

CAmpbell John Coats, of Clathick, merchant, Virginia ſtreet.

Campbell and Ingram, merchants and inſurance brokers, Exchange.

Campbell John and Co. inſurance brokers, Exchange.

Campbell John and Co. merchants, Argyle ſtreet.

Campbell John, ditto. Jamaica ſtreet.

Campbell John, ditto. Maidera court.

Campbell Colin, ditto. Jamaica ſtreet.

Campbell Archibald, ditto. Gallowgate.

Campbell George, ditto. Gibſon's wynd.

Campbell Alexander, ditto. high ſtreet.

Campbell John, Stockwell ſugar houſe.

Carrick Robert, merchant, ſhip bank,

Carmichael William, ditto. Stockwell.

Coulters James, ditto. bridgegate.

Coulters Laurence, ditto. ditto.

Corbet Cuningham, and Co. ditto. Jamaica ſtrt.

Cowan Andrew, ditto. Grahameſtown.

Cooper William and Alex. ditto. high ſtreet.

Colquhoun Hugh, ditto. King's ſtreet.

Colquhoun Walter, ditto. Millar ſtreet.

Colquhoun Shiels and Co. yarn merchants high ſtreet.

Colquhoun John, merchant, Trongate.

Clark William, ditto. Queen's ſtreet.

Connel James. ditto. high ſtreet.

Coats William, ditto. Gallowgate.

Coats John, ditto. Dowhill.

Crawford George, ditto. Queen's ſtreet.

Crawford, Robert and Co. foap work, head of
Candleriggs.

Crawford Robert of Poftle, merchant, Bell's
wynd.

Crawford Matthew, yarn merchant, ditto.

Craigie Laurence, merchant high ftreet.

Craig William, timber merchant, Clyde ftreet.

Craig William, merchant, entry to St Andrew's
church.

Crofs Hugh, and Co. infurance brokers, Trongate.

Crofs David, merchant, Adam's court.

Cuningham William and Co. merchants› Queen's
ftreet.

Currie John, Currie's clofs high ftreet.

Chambers Mr, preacher of the Gofpel, Dowhill.

Carlyle John, collector of the cefs, Legat's land,
high ftreet.

Carrick James and Alexander, woolen and linen
drapers, high ftreet.

Cameron Hector, ditto. Gallowgate.

Carmichael Hugh, ditto. King's ftreet.

Campbell Patrick and Co. ditto. ditto.

Clark Donald, ditto. Trongate.

Craig Robert, ditto. King's ftreet.

Cuthbertfon and Sym, whole fale linen drapers,
high ftreet.

Campbell James, manufacturer, grammar fchool
wynd.

Carmichael Duncan, thread manufacturer, blackfriars wynd.

Chalmers Alexander, incle manufacturer, Dowhill.

Coats John, ditto. Grammar fchool wynd.

Clawfon Jafper, Stockwell fugar houfe.

Carmichael James and George, grocers and ſpirit dealers, head of Salt market.

Carſwell Allan, ditto. near foot of ditto.

Campbell Mr feed ſhop, Trongate.

Campbell Andrew, ſpirit dealer, ditto.

Chriſtie Miſs, grocer and ſpirit dealer, ditto.

Chriſtie David, ditto. high ſtreet.

Colquhouns, ditto. Trongate.

Clachan William, ditto. high ſtreet-

Cochran John, ditto. ditto.

Crum John, grocer and cotton dealer, Gallow- gate.

Chriſtie and Smith, tobacconiſts, Trongate.

Campbell James, ſadler, ditto.

Calder John, watch and clock maker, high ſtreet.

Campbell John, ditto. and billet maſter, Gallow- gate.

Craig James and John, iron mongers, Salt market.

Craig Andrew, ditto. Trongate.

Connel Matthew, copper and white iron ſmith, bridgegate.

Cullen James, ſilver ſmith, back of tontine.

Cullen Daniel, ſtamp maſter, high ſtreet.

Collins Edward and Richard, paper makers and bleachers, dalmuir.

Campbell Joſhua, teacher of muſic, high ſtreet.

Campbell James, ditto. ditto.

Campbell James, teacher of dancing, Gallowgate

Chapman and Duncan, Printers of the Glaſgow mercury, Trongate.

Coubrough Archibald, bookſeller, high ſtreet.

Colvill Robert, book binder, Trongate.

Craig John and Robert, bakers and victualers, Trongate.

Craig Robert, baker ditto.

Campbell Archibald, baker, Bell's wynd.
Campbell John, ditto. King's ſtreet.
Cuthbertſon William, brewer, calton.
Campbell Daniel, inn keeper, oroom o'law.
Cairns David, ditto Argyle ſtreet.
Clydeſdale John, ditto. Bun's wynd.
Cochran John, ditto. Salt market.
Crawford Charles ditto. Bell's wynd.
Chambers Thomas, taylor, gallowgate,
Clark John, ditto. Trongate.
Couper John, ditto, high ſtreet.
Currie John, ditto. Gallowgate.
Chapman John, teacher of Engliſh, high ſtreet.
Chriſtie Alex. ditto. Salt market.
Campbell Alex. teacher of fencing, high ſtreet.
Carſe John, barber, high ſtreet.
Caſſels John, ditto. ditto.
Colvill Stephen, ditto. Bell's wynd,
Crawford Charles, head of Jamaica ſtreet.
Campbell Peter, tallow chandler, King's ſtreet.
Campbell James, tanner, dowhill.
Clarke John, tanner, Gallowgate.
Caldwall Andrew, ſhoe maker, Salt market.
Calder Robert, ditto. high ſtreet.
Campbell John, ditto. Gibſon's wynd.
Carmichael William, ditto. Salt market.
Clark James, dito. Trongate.
Cuningham Charles, leather cutter, gallowgate.
Clark James, coach maker, ditto.
Clark David, ditto. ditto.
Cameron Alex. hammerman. Salt market.
Craig John, ditto. Trongate.
Crichton James, ditto. grammar ſchool wynd.
Crighton John, ditto Salt market.
Craig James, Plummer, clyde ſtreet.
Caiton David, wright, Stockwell.
Campbell Alex. ditto. ditto.

Cocke Robert, wright. Trongate.
Craig Robert, cooper, Stockwell.
Chriſtie Thomas, painter, ditto.
Cleland Matthew, maſon, Salt market.
Cleland James, hoſier, gallowgate.
Campbell Hugh, ditto. grammar ſchool wynd.
Cooper John, ditto. old wynd.
Campbell Duncan, gardner, gallowgate.
Cowan William, ditto. Argyle ſtreet.
Callan James, high ſtreet
Carmichael Robert, lets lodgings, gallowgate.
Craig Robert, keeper of bridewell, drygate.
Crofs Robert, college ſervitor.
Cuningham James, ſheriff officer, Salt market.
Croſby John, Hamilton poſt. ditto.
Clark Donald, boatman, broom o'law.

D

DALE David, yarn merchant, high ſtreet.
    Denniſtown James, ſenior, merchant, Queen's ſtreet.
Denniſtown James, junior, ditto. Argyle ſtreet.
Dechman James, gallowgate.
Dinwiddie Robert, merchant, Germiſtown.
Donald Robert, merchant.
Donald Thomas, ditto. Stockwell.
Donaldſon and Dinwiddie, ditto. high ſtreet.
Douglas William and James, ditto. Argyle ſtrèet.
Douglas John, ditto. miller's ſtreet.
Douglas Colin of mains, Horn's land Argyle ſtreet.
Douglas William, merchant, ditto.
Dreghorn Robert of Roughill, clyde ſtreet.

Dunmore Thomas, merchant, horn's land Argyle ftreet.

Dunmore Robert and Co. ditto. miller's ftreet.

Dunlop James of Garnkirk, ditto. Argyle ftreet.

Dunlop Thomas, ditto. Trongate.

Dunlop William, ditto. Queen's ftreet.

Dunlop John, ditto. ditto.

Dunlop Robert, infurance office exchange.

Duguid John, King's ftreet fugar houfe.

Duguid William, ditto.

Dalziel Mrs, Mr Dreghorn's land Stockwell.

Dewar Andrew, cafhier, merchant bank, Maxwell's ftreet.

Donaldfon Alex. teller, fhip bank high ftreet.

Dennifton James, woolen and linen draper, high ftreet.

Donald William, wholefale linen draper, gallowgate.

Dunlop and Wilfon, woolen and linen drapers, ditto.

Donaldfon James fenior, keeps a callender, Crofs well high ftreet.

Donaldfon James junior, King's ftreet.

Dunlop and Wilfon, bookfellers, Trongate.

Duncan James fenior, ditto. oppofite the guard Trongate.

Duncan James junior, ditto. Salt market.

Duncan Robert, printer, ditto.

Duncan John, bookbinder, ditto.

Duncan John of milnfield, proprietor of fnuff mills &c.

Dalrymple David and Co. hofiers, back of the exchange.

Douglas Andrew, ditto. Salt market.

Douglas William, ditto. bridgegate.

Dunlop Alexander, ditto. Gallowgate.

Dow John, one of the mafters of the grammar fchool, grammar fchool wynd.

Dickfon Gilbert, teacher of languages.

Dickfon William, ditto. of Englifh, gibfon's wynd.

Dick Alex teacher of dancing, Trongate.

Dickfon Robert, iron monger, King's ftreet.

Dalnotter iron work Company's ware houfe Stockwell.

Dougal James, grocer and fpirit dealer, Salt market.

Dun James, ditto. oppofite the guard, Trongate.

Drew John, ditto. wynd head.

Dobbie Mr. fugar boyler, Candleriggs.

Dick William and Andrew, tobacconifts, high ftreet.

Dinning Robert, ditto. gallowgate.

Dick William, gives out tickets for the Edinburgh fly, Trongate.

Dunbar Andrew, vintner, ditto.

Durie Thomas, ditto, ditto.

Downie Robert, inn-keeper, gallowgate.

Drew John, ditto Argyle ftreet.

Dalmahoy Alex. faddler, bridgegate.

Dalgleifh David, manufaѐturer, drygate.

Dun Malcom, ditto dilto.

Dun Henderfon and Co. hard wood dealers, gallowgate.

Dallas Alex. wright, Jamaica ftreet.

Duncan William, ditto. high ftreet.

Dun William, ditto. Maxwell ftreet.

Dun William, wheel wright, high ftreet.

Downie Robert, wright Salt market.

Duncan Andrew, baker, Trongate.

Duncan Andrew, ditto. Candlerigs.

Darling William, taylor, gallowgate.

Dow Dougal, ditto. Trongate.

Dunlop James, taylor, King's ftreet.
Douglas Archibald, ftay maker, Salt market.
Dallas John, copper and white iron fmith, King's ftreet.
Duncan William, ditto. bridgegate.
Dickfon James, hammerman, Candlerigs.
Dick William, ditto. King's ftreet.
Dickie Andrew, ditto. Salt market.
Draper James, ditto. ditto.
Douglas George, plummer, Argyle ftreet.
Dick William iron-monger, bridgegate.
Duff John, at Smithfield Company's ware houfe, broom o'law.
Dinwiddie Laurence, fhoe maker, King's ftreet.
Douglas William, ditto. new wynd.
Dunbar William, ditto. King's ftreet.
Dickfon Robert, barber, Argyle ftreet.
Dickfon John, clothlapper, Gallowgate.
Drape John, hatt maker, Trongate.
Dainty Captain, Grahame's fquare.
Duncan John, merchant, grammar fchool wynd.
Dempfter Anthony, painter, gallowgate.
Dempfter John, porter to the Thiftle bank.
Dillon Lind, plaifterer, bridgegate.
Donald John, maltman, Argyle ftreet.
Douglas Robert, gardner, rottenrow.
Drummond Robert, tallow chandler, high ftreet.
Drummond Alex flax dreffer, Bell's wynd.
Durie Robert, reed maker, high ftreet.
Dun John, fifh hook maker, Trongate.
Dunlop James, dyer fpout mouth.

E

Edmifton, Lothian and Co. merchants, high ftreet.

Edmond David, fenior, merchant, Salt market.

Edmond David, junior, cotton dealer, ditto.

Erfkine Michael, infurance office, exchange.

Elliot David, merchant, Jamaica ftreet.

Ewing Walter and Co, ditto. Trongate.

Ewing Stevenfon and Co. dry falters, ditto.

Ewing and Galloway, woolen and linen drapers, Trongate.

Ewing Alexander, ditto. ditto.

Ewing Andrew, ditto. ditto

Ewing Patrick, ditto. ditto.

Ewing James, grocer and fpirit dealer high ftreet.

Edgar Thomas, ditto. Trongate.

Eglinton and Wotherfpoon, ditto. Gallowgate.

Erfkine Ralph and Co. ditto. Trongate.

Erfkine George, preacher of the Gofpel, Bun' wynd.

Ewing Robert, baker and victualer, Trongate.

Edmond James, baker Stockwell.

Elder John, cordner and fpirit dealer, gibfon's wynd.

Eadie John, cork cutter and vintner, Trongate.

Eaton William, hofier, grammar fchool wynd.

Edgar William, brufh maker, havanna ftreet.

Edwards William, engraver, Salt market.

Edwards Alex. barber high ftreet.

Edwards James, ditto. ditto.

Edwards Thomas, horfe fetter, Candlerigs.

Ewing John, wright, high ftreet.

F

FInlay Robert and Co. merchants, Miller
    ſtreet.
Finlay James, ditto. Bell's wynd.
French William, ditto. Queen's ſtreet.
Fleming Mrs. Miller's ſtreet.
Freeland John and Co. yarn merchants, high
    ſtreet.
Falconer Thomas, woolen and linen draper, Tron-
    gate.
Ferguſon Andrew, ditto. ditto.
Ferguſon Duncan, ditto. king's ſtreet.
Ferguſon Duncan, ditto. high ſtreet.
Ferguſon James, ditto. gallowgate.
Ferguſon John, ditto. high ſtreet.
Forreſt and Steel, ditto. gallowgate.
Forreſter Robert, yarn merchant, high ſtreet.
Farie Robert, bookſeller, Salt market.
Fleming William, ditto. ditto.
Foulis Andrew, Printer to the Univerſity, high
    ſtreet.
Ferguſon Hector, manufacturer, new wynd
Fergus, James, ditto. moodie's yard.
Fleeming John, ditto. dowhill.
Fouls John, ditto. gallowgate.
Freebairn John, ditto. ditto.
Forlong James, ditto. havanna ſtreet.
Forlong William, merchant bank.
Fleeming David, junior, and Co. iron mongers,
    Trongate.
Foreſter and Reid, hardwaremen, ditto.

Fifher Alex. tobacconift, Trongate.

Fifher John, ditto. bridgegate.

Fifcfher William, teacher of languages and vintner, Salt market.

Finlayfon James, teacher of Englifh, high ftreet.

Frazer William, teacher of dancing, king's ftreet.

Fergufon Alex. grocer and fpirit dealer, gallow-gate.

Foreft James, fpirit dealer, ditto.

Fleckefield Thomas, grocer and fpirit dealer, A-dam's court.

Finlay William, inn-keeper, Trongate.

Foulis John, ditto. King's ftreet.

Freeland John, ditto. high ftreet.

Falconer Peter, wright, Stockwell.

Finlay John, ditto. havanna ftreet.

Finlay John, ditto. Stockwell.

Finlay George, ditto. high ftreet.

Forrefter Walter, ditto. gallowgate.

Farie John, baker, Stockwell.

Fleeming William. ditto gallowgate.

Farquhar Alex. taylor and vintner Trongate

Fergus Alex. taylor, Salt market.

Forrefter David, ditto. Trongate.

Foreft Alex. fhoe maker, ditto.

Fullerton William, ditto. high ftreet.

Fergus Thomas, dryfalter, Salt market.

Fergus John, Mr Bogle's brewery Candlerigs.

Fleeming William, copper and white iron fmith, gallowgate.

Fulton William, hammerman, Trongate.

Farie Robert, comb maker, gallowgate.

Finlay William gardner, ditto.

Fleeming John, flefher, king's ftreet.

Ford John, fifh hook maker, bridgegate.

Foreft William, hofier, old venal.

Foot Thomas, cooper, bridgegate.
French James, dyer, Dowhill.
Freebairn John, Boatman broom o'law.

X X X X X X X X X X X X X

G

GLasford John, of Dougalſtown merchant, Trongate.
Gordon James, ditto Argyle ſtreet.
Govan Archibald, ditto miller's ſtreet.
Gray John, ditto Salt market.
Gibſon John, accountant, ditto.
Grahame Archibald, caſhier thiſtle bank, Virginia ſtreet.
Grinlay Alex. merchant, high ſtreet.
Grinlay James, yarn merchant, ditto.
Gardner William and Co. whole ſale linen printers. Bell's wynd.
Good, Macbrayne, and Co. ditto high ſtreet.
Grant, Wood, and Co, carpet manufactory, foot of havanna ſtreet.
Gardner Moſes, manufacturer, at Mr Stirling's, high ſtreet.
Glen Alex. ſilk ditto Trongate.
Glen James, whole ſale linen merchant, Salt market.
Glen Zacharias, Stockwell.
Glen James, writer, at Mr Claud Marſhall's, laigh kirk cloſs.
Gould John, manufacturer, havanna ſtreet.
Goudie John, ditto ditto.
Graham John, ditto high ſtreet.
Graham James, ditto ditto.
Galbraith Walter, hoſier, ditto.

Girdwood Alex. woolen and linen draper, gallowgate.

Gilfillan Thomas' ditto Trongate.

Gilfillan and Galbraith, ditto high ftreet.

Glen William, ditto Trongate.

Govan Alex. ditto King's ftreet

Goudilock William, ditto ditto.

Graham and Wardrop, ditto ditto.

Grieve John and Co. ditto gallowgate.

Grieve Adam, Bridgegate.

Grieve Mrs, makes gum flowers, &c. ditto.

Gray and Donald, haberdafhers, Trongate.

Galt John, teacher of Englifh, Hutchiefon's hofpital.

Gibfon John, teacher of writing, &c. Trongate.

Gordon William, teacher of the mathematicks.

Gould William, teacher of mufic, high ftreet.

Gardner John, mathematical inftrument maker, Bell's wynd.

Gemmel Robert, tobacconift, Salt market

George James, ditto Bridgegote.

Graham Walter, ditto. high ftreet.

Galloway Alex. fpirit dealer, Broom o'law.

Galloway John, grocer and fpirit dealer, gallowgate.

Galloway and Buchanan, ditto Salt market.

Gardner John, wright and fpirit dealer, old toll. gallowgate.

Galbraith James, ditto. gallowgate.

Gardner Thomas, ditto. Trongate.

Gardner Robert, ditto high ftreet.

Gardner Adam, ditto ditto.

Gemmil Hugh, ditto Trongate.

Gilfillan James, ditto high ftreet.

Glafs Hugh, ditto Salt market.

Gilmour Allan, ditto Brigdegate.

Gilchrift and Co's. china and glafs fhop Tron-
gate.
Gray John, fpirit dealer, Stockwell.
Gray James, grocer and fpirit dealer, high ftreet.
Grant John, grocer and falt office, King's ftreet.
Galloway Alex. inn-keeper, Bridgegate.
Gardner Archibald, ditto gallowgate.
Gardner Alex. ditto Candlerigs.
Gardner William, ditto high ftreet.
Gourlay Mrs. vintner, Salt market.
Gemmil William, ditto gallowgate.
Gyles Samuel, inn-keeper Trongate.
Graham George, merchant, gallowgate.
Graham Adam, gold fmith and jeweler, King's
ftreet.
Gray Robert, ditto Trongate.
Graham and Wardrop, copper and white iron
fmiths, king's ftreet.
Grant Eaglesfield, wire worker, Trongate.
Gibfon James, wright, gallowgate.
Glen and Scot, ditto Bell's wynd.
Gordon William, ditto Salt market.
Graham James, ditto bridgegate.
Gibfon David, clerk to the weighoufe.
Galloway Robert, baker, Argyle ftreet.
Gentles William, ditto high ftreet.
Gibb Archibald, ditto ditto.
Graham John. ditto Candlerigs.
Graham James, ditto Trongate.
Gardner John, taylor, gallowgate.
Gilmour John, ditto Trongate.
Graham Mr. ditto Bell's wynd.
Gilchrift M. fhoe fhop, Trongate.
Galloway Robert, fhoe maker, high ftreet.
Gillies John, ditto Bridgegate.
Gray James, ditto Salt market.

Gilchrift William, horfe fetter, Trongate.
Greenfield William, ditto ditto.
Gall Thomas, barber, Bridgegate.
Gilfillan John, ditto gallowgate.
Gibfon John, Flefher, Bridgegate.
Gilmour Alex ditto new wynd.
Galt James, cork cutter, Trongate.
Gardner James, comb maker, gallowgate.
Galbraith Jofeph, Printer, high ftreet.
Gillies James, bookfeller, ditto.
Gillies Alex. confectioner, gallowgate.
Glafgow Journal printing office, Gibfon's clofs.
Girvan John, Broom o'law.
Gillefpie John, hammerman, Trongate.
Gilmour Arthur, bottle work, Broom o'law
Gilchrift Robert, boatman, ditto.
Gilchrift William, ditto ditto.
Gardner James, Paifley poft, back wynd.

H

HAmilton and Brown, infurance office, Ex-
change.
Hamilton James, ditto ditto.
Hamilton and Wilfon, ditto Trongrate.
Hamilton James, merchant, Jamaica ftreet.
Hamilton Gilbert, Carron ware houfe, Queen's
ftreet.
Hamilton John of Barn's, merchant, Argyle
ftreet.
Hamilton John junior, ditto Trongate.
Hamilton Archibald, ditto Stockwell.

Hamilton Archibald, merchant, king's ſtreet.

Hardie, Millar, and Co. whole ſale linen drapers, Bell's wynd.

Henderſon William, Bottle work, Broom o'law.

Henderſon Archibald, merchant, Argyle ſtreet.

Hill James, writer, Trongate.

Hill Thomas, accountant, Trongate.

Hopkirk James, merchant, Argyle ſtreet.

Hopkirk Thomas, ditto ditto.

Howſtoun Andrew of Jordanhill, ditto ditto.

Howſtoun Robert, ditto ditto.

Howſtoun Thomas, London porter cellar, Stock-well.

Hunter James, merchant, Donald's land Trongate.

Hunter William, ditto Jamaica ſtreet.

Hutton James, ditto Queen's ſtreet.

Henderſon Thomas, timber merchant weſt end of canal.

Henderſon, Dun and Co. hard wood merchant's, Gallowgate.

Harper William and ſon, lawn and cambric manufacturers, high ſtreet.

Hadden John, manufacturer, Gallowgate.

Henry Alex. ditto Bell's wynd.

Herdman James, ditto ditto.

Herbertſon John, thread manufacturer, Rotten-row.

Hervey Alex. incle manufacturer, foot of the Salt market.

Hervey William, ditto high ſtreet.

Henderſon John, ditto grammar ſchool wynd.

Hall James, hoſier, king's ſtreet.

Hails John, ditto Gallowgate.

Hannah James, ditto Bridgegate.

Hepburn Robert, ditto king's ſtreet.

Houſhold George, ſugar boiler, king's St ſugar houſe.

Harvie Andrew, woolen and linen draper, Trongate.

Hart Walter, ditto Gallowgate.

Hamilton John, youngeſt, ditto ditto.

Hume Mrs, millener, Argyle ſtreet.

Harvie James, grocer and ſpirit dealer, Trongate.

Harvie Robert, ditto Bridgegate.

Hamilton John, ditto king's ſtreet.

Hardy John, ditto Stockwell.

Hay Barclay and Co. tallow chandlers, king's ſtreet.

Hamilton George, wright, high ſtreet.

Hamilton John, ditto. Gallowgate.

Hay John, ditto high ſtreet.

Horn William, ditto Argyle ſtreet.

Hogg William, ditto Grammar ſchool wynd.

Hunter James, ditto Stockwell.

Houſhold John, cooper, ditto.

Hoods John, ditto Candlerigs.

Hoods Andrew, ditto Gallowgate.

Hamilton John, watch and clock maker, ditto.

Henry David, ſadler, ditto.

Heron Peter, vintner black bull inn Argyle ſtreet.

Harvie Mrs. ditto Trongate.

Hamilton Thomas, ditto king's ſtreet,

Hamilton James, ditto high ſtreet.

Hunter Robert, ditto Salt market.

Hunter Robert, ditto Gallowgate.

Howſton John, keeps a livery ſtable, Argyle ſtreet.

Hamilton Alex. tobacconiſt, Stockwell.

Hardy James, ditto high ſtreet.

Hardy Robert, baker, ditto.

Hatridge Andrew, barber, Trongate.

Haddin John barber and inn-keeper, Bridge-gate·

Henderſon David, barber, Candlerigs.

Hardy John, taylor, Grammar ſchool wynd.

Herbertſon William, ditto Bridgegate.

Hutchieſon William, ditto Salt market.

Harvie Mrs. Stay maker, Trongate.

Hay William, hinge maker, Cowcaddens.

Hood John, hammerman, high ſtreet.

Hood Andrew, ditto ditto.

Hunter Charles, ditto Candlerigs.

Hutchieſon George, ditto Grammar ſchool wynd.

Hannah Robert, hard ware man, Salt market.

Hutcheſon Charles, bookſeller, ditto.

Hutcheſon Alex. book binder, ditto.

Heugh Walter, ditto ditto.

Henderſon James, teacher of dancing, Gallow-gate.

Hunter Joſeph, teacher of Engliſh, Bell's wynd.

Hardy Andrew, dyer, Argyle ſtreet.

Hutton John, ditto Virginia ſtreet.

Harvie Alex. ſhoe maker, Salt market.

Halliday Arthur, pipe maker, high ſtreet.

Hamilton James, confectioner, Trongate.

Hogg Andrew, reed maker, Bridgegate.

Hogg John, boatman, Broom o'law.

J

Jackſon James, Poſt maſter, Jamaica ſtreet,

Ingram William, merchant, Charlotte ſtreet.

Johnſton, Bannatine, and Co. hoſiers, Trongate

Johnſton Joſhua, merchant, Gallowgate.

Jack Alex. teacher of writing, Gallowgate.
Irvine Dr. chymiſt, high ſtreet.
Irvine and Blackie, tobacconiſts, Salt market.
Jack Thomas, manufacturer, new wynd.
Jamiſon William, ditto Grammar ſchool wynd.
Jamiſon John and ſon, looking glaſs makers, king's
    ſtreet.
Jamiſon John, ſtocking dealer, high ſtreet.
Jarvies Robert, woolen draper, ditto.
Jaffrey James, wright, Charlotte ſtreet.
Jarvie John, vintner, baſon inn weſt end of the
    canal.
Jenkin John, ſhoe maker, Bell's wynd.
Jenkin John, taylor, high ſtreet.
Ingles Thomas, hatt maker, Trongate.
Ingles Peter, hoſier,   wynd.
Innes William, grocer and ſpirit dealer, Tron-
    gate.
Innes Charles, plaiſterer, Stockwell.
Imrie John, tallow chandler, Bridgegate.
Johnſton John, Smithfield, Broom o'law.

K

KIppen George, merchant, entry to St An-
    drew's church, Salt market.
Kinnibrugh and Todd, yarn merchants, high
    ſtreet.
Kemp Charles, manufacturer and bleacher, Sauchi-
    hall.
Kenon James, cotton manufacturer, Gallowgate.
Kirkland John, manufacturer, high ſtreet.
Kirkland James, thread ditto calton.

Kennedy Daniel, linen draper, high ftreet.
Knox George, woolen and linen draper, Tron-
gate.
Ker John, grocer and fpirit dealer, high ftreet.
Kirkwood James, ditto Trongate.
Kirkland John, ditto Bridgegate.
Knox Robert, ditto and gun powder office, Stock-
well.
Ker John, watch and clock maker, Salt market.
Kirkland James, ditto Trongate.
Kirkwood James, fadler, Argyle ftreet.
Ker Archibald, taylor, Bridgegate.
Kinnibrugh Thomas, ditto Candlerigs.
King John, flefher, Bridgegate:
Kirkpatrick William, ditto back wynd.
Kippen William, inn-keeper, Gallowgate.
Kirkland Matthew, ditto Salt market.
Kay Jahn, wright, maxwell ftreet.
Ker Mifs, lets lodgings, head of old wynd.
King Robert, mafon, Gallowgate.
King John, barber, Argyle ftreet.
Kinnarid George, ftabler, ditto.

L

Lang, Auchinclofs, and Co. merchants, Gal-
lowgate:
Lang William, keeps callander, ditto.
Laird James, merchant, Jamaica ftreet.
Lawrie John, ditto Gallowgate.
Lawrie William, agent, weft end of Great Canal.
Leitch and Smith, merchants, Trongate.
Lightbody John and Adam, ditto Bell's wynd.
F

Lindſay James and Co. timber merchants, Broom o'law.

Lowdown, Craigie, and Co. merchants high ſtrt.

Lockhart, Monteath, and Co. lawn and cambric manufacturers, Trongate.

Lockhart James, hard ware man, Salt market.

Lockhart James, haberdaſher, ditto.

Logans Miſs, milleners, King's ſtreet.

Lang James, woolen draper, high ſtreet.

Leitch James, woolen and linen draper, Trongate.

Lindſay James, ditto ditto.

Lang William, manufacturer, Dowhill.

Lennox David, ditto Rottenrow.

Leitch John, thread manufacturer, Salt market.

Laroch Mr. French teacher, Gibſon's wynd.

Laird Daniel, grocer and ſpirit dealer, Salt market.

Lowrie Wiliam, grocer and ſpirit dealer, Salt market.

Lowrie Mrs. ditto Gallowgate.

Lowric Thomas, entry to St Andrew's church.

Lobon George, ditto Trongate.

Lang Robert, dry ſalter, Salt market.

Lang William, hatt maker, ditto.

Lang James, copper and white iron ſmith, Bridgegate.

Lang William, hammerman, old wynd.

Lamb James, ditto high ſtreet.

Leechman William, ditto ditto.

Leechman John, ditto Gallowgate.

Lindſay Patrick, copper and white iron ſmith, high ſtreet.

Lumiſden James, engraver, Trongate.

Lindſay David, wright, new wynd.

Logan John, ditto Adam's court.

Lyon Richard, wright, new wynd.
Lillie John, taylor, high ſtreet.
Luke Michael, ditto gibſon's land Salt market.
Lindſay Walter, barber, Gibſon's wynd.
Logie Robert, ditto high ſtreet.
Logie William, ditto ditto.
Lamont John, baker, Gallowgate.
Lindſay Patrick, ditto Candlerigs.
Lang John, fleſher, new wynd.
Lawſon David, ditto ditto.
Lawſon Thomas, ditto Bridgegate.
Lawſon John, jailor, high ſtreet.
Lawſon Andrew, maſon, Jamaica ſtreet.
Lawſon Ralph, broker, Gallowgate.
Lawſon Mrs, glove maker, ditto.
Lapſley William, inn-keeper, Argyle ſtreet.
Lockhart John. ditto Stockwell.
Lang Claud, boatman, Broom o'law.
Lindſay Andrew, ditto ditto.
Love Daniel, ditto Doghouſe.
Lees James, ſhoe maker, Gibſon's wynd.
Leckie William, Gallowgate.
Liſter James, plaſterer, maxwell's ſtreet.
Logan Robert, ſadler, high ſtreet.

❉❉❉❉❉❉❉❉❉❉❉❉❉❉❉❉❉❉❉

M

MAxwell Sir James, James Ritchie, and Co.
Thiſtle bank, Virginia ſtreet.
Merchant Banking Company, head of maxwell's
ſtreet.
Moores, Carrick, and Co. ſhip bank, Argyle
ſtreet.

Marſhall Robert, merchant, Glaſgow tanwork, Gallowgate.

Maſon John, merchant, Trongate.

M'Caull George and Co. inſurance office, ditto.

M'Caull James, merchant, foot of Argyle ſtreet.

M'Caull Mr. ditto millar ſtreet.

M'Creddy Archibald, ditto ditto.

M'Cerddy and Miller, proprietors of marble manufactory, Queen's ſtreet.

M'Come Hector, merchant, Trongate.

M'Alpine, Fleming and Co. whole ſale linen printers, Bell's wynd.

M'Alpine John, merchant, beyond old Gallowgate toll.

M'Auſlan Robert, tan work, high ſtreet.

M'Dowall John, merchant, Dunlop ſtreet.

M'Dowall James, ditto horn's land, Argyle ſtreet.

M'Gregor James junior, ditto Candlerigs.

M'Intoſh Murdoch and Co. merchants, Trongate.

M'Indoe John, ditto Gallowgate.

M'Farlane James, ditto Trongate.

M'Leans, M'Kay, and Co. ditto ditto.

M'Lellan Hugh, ditto Queen's ſtreet.

M'Nea John, ditto ditto.

Miller John of Weſtertown, ditto millar ſtreet.

Miller George and Co. ditto Gallowgate.

Miller James junior, ditto Bell's wynd.

Miller John of Wellhouſe, Gallowgate.

Miller Andrew, yarn merchant, high ſtreet.

Mitchel James, merchant, ditto.

Monteath Walter, ditto Horn's land Argyle ſtreet.

Morton James, ditto ditto.

Murdoch, Warroch, and Co. great brewerie, Anderſtown.

Murdoch Peter, merchant Queen's ſtreet.

Murdoch James, merchant, Tenants houſe, beyond Gallowgate toll.

Munn Alex. ditto Jamaica ſtreet.

Monro Alex. ditto Stockwell.

Maxwell and Smith, writers, Argyle ſtreet.

Maxwell and Grahame, ditto ditto.

Marſhall Samnel, woolen and linen draper, King's
ſtreet.

M'Culloch John, ditto Trongate.

M'Corkindale Duncan, ditto ditto.

M'Caw Robert, ditto high ſtreet.

M'Farlane William, ditto Trongate.

M'Gilvra Malcom and Co. ditto high ſtrect.

M'Kechnie John, ditto Trongate.

M'Kean Alex. ditto ditto.

M'Lintock Robert junior, ditto high ſtreet.

M'Indoe Alex. ditto ditto.

M'Indoe Robert, ſilk mercer and haberdaſher,
Argyle ſtreet.

M'Kinzie, Matthew and Co. woolen and linen
drapers, Trongate.

M'Vickar John, ditto high ſtreet.

Muir John ſenior, ditto Trongate.

Muir John junior and Co. ditto Gallowgate.

Mutter Thomas, ditto Salt market.

Miller, Shirra, and Co. haberdaſhers, Gallowgate.

Miller George and William, ditto Trongate.

Mudie William, ditto. Trongate.

M'Haffie David, ditto Gallowgate.

Miller and Ewing, woolen and linen drapers,
ditto.

M'Aulay Walter, hardware dealer, Salt market

M'Donald Angus and Co. jewellery and toy ware
room, head of Salt market.

M'Donald Angus, hard ware and toy ſhop, ditto.

M'Kean James, ditto ditto.

M'Nair James, ditto ditto.

M'Ewen James, gold fmith and jeweler, King's ftreet.

Milne and Campbell, ditto Trongate.

Muir Hugh and George, hard ware men and jewelers, King's ftreet.

Mair Archibald, upholftery ware - room, Salt market.

Mann William and Co. ditto Trongate.

Martin Ure and Co. ditto ditto.

M'Kenzie and Co. ditto ditto.

M'Arthur John, land furveyor, Keppochill.

M'Arthur William, paper maker, Dawfholm.

M'Gown Archibald, bookfeller, head of Stockwell,

M'Nair John, ditto Trongate.

Montgomery Daniel, ditto Gibfon's wynd.

Mennons John, printer of the Glafgow Mercury, Salt market.

Marfhall John, book binder, high ftreet.

M'Nair Robert, ditto Salt market.

M'Pherfon Evan, ditto ditto.

Millar Ebenezer, ditto ditto.

M'Brair Archibald, dry falter, high ftreet.

Maxwell Robert, ditto Gallowgate

M'Lintock Robert fenior, ditto Trongate.

M'Nair Robert, eafter fugar houfe, Gallowgate.

M'Alafter Robert, manufacturer, new vennal.

M'Kean Andrew, lawn and cambric manufacturer, high ftreet.

M'Kerow Hugh, thread manufacturer, ditto.

M'Nair Robert, manufacturer, old wynd.

Miller Richard, ditto Salt market.

Miller Mofes, ditto high ftreet.

Miller Thomas, ditto Grammar fchool wynd.

Monteath James and fons, ditto high ftreet.

Morrifon James, lawn and cambric manufacturer, Claythorn.

Murdoch and Love, ditto Caftle pens land, high ftreet.

Muir Robert, manufacturer, ditto.

Murchie William, ditto havanna ftreet.

Mair Charles, hofier, Gallowgate.

M'Millan Robert, ditto high ftreet.

M'Millan Andrew, ditto ditto.

M'Nab Duncan, ditto Trongate.

M'Kinzie James, ditto Galowgate.

Morris Robert and Co. ditto high ftreet.

M'Grigor Alex. hatt maker, Salt market.

M'Kinlay and Boyle, ditto ditto.

M'Arthur Daniel, one of the mafters of the Grammar fchool, Trongate.

M'Kinzie John, teacher of Englifh, hutchiefon's hofpital.

M'Kinlay William, ditto new wynd.

M'Ilquham Robert, ditto broad clofs high ftreet.

Monach James, teacher of writing, &c. Trongate.

Meickle John, tobacconift Gallowgate.

Muir and Kirkland, ditto ditto.

M'Arthur Peter, druggift, Trongate.

Moncrief and Company's laboratory, King's ftreet.

Mackie Robert, grocer and fpirit dealer, Bridgegate.

Mann David, ditto Gallowgate.

Matthie Mrs. ditto high ftreet.

Marfhall John, china and ftone ware dealer, King's fteeet.

M'Allum James, grocer and fpirit dealer, high ftreet.

M'Adam William, ditto wynd head, ditto.

M'Donald John, grocer and ſpirit dealer, Tron-
gate.
M'Innes Daniel, ditto Bridgegate.
Malcolm and Buchanan, ditto Gallowgate.
Meikle Matthew, ditto King's ſtreet.
Miller Mrs. ditto Gallowgate.
Miller John, ditto Gibſon's wynd.
Miller William, ditto Candlerigs.
Muir James, ditto and hop merchant, high ſtreet.
Mungal Robert, grocer and ſpirit dealer, ditto.
Morton Alex. ditto Gallowgate.
Moore Edward, ditto Salt market.
M'Auſlan and Auſtin, feed and nurſery men,
Trongate.
M'Alpin and Co. tallow chandlers, Salt market.
M'Allum Mr. ditto high ſtreet.
M'Kellar Duncan, ditto Trongate.
M'Nair James, ditto ditto.
Mann Robert wright, Stockwell.
Martin William, wright, Bridgegate,
Martin Alex. ditto ditto.
M'Alaſter Walter, ditto Bell's wynd.
M'Aulay John, ditto Jamaica ſtreet.
M'Farlane Peter, ditto Bridgegate.
M'Whannel Edward. ditto St Enochs wynd.
Miller David, ditto Garſcube bridge
Morris John, ditto Gallowgate.
Morriſon John, ditto Argyle ſtreet.
Murray William, ditto ditto.
Murray Maurice. ditto ditto.
Murdoch Alex. ditto Goose dubbs.
M'Viccar Niel, carpenter, Bridgegate.
M'Kell John, miln wright, Trongate.
Meikle William, plaiſterer, maxwell's ſtreet,
Miller Alex. ſenior, Slater, old wynd.
Miller Alex. junior, ditto ditto.

M'Arthur Duncan, cooper, Bridgegate.
M'Kinnon Norman, ditto Argyle ſtreet.
M'Alpin Daniel, baker, Bridgegate.
M'Crocket Boyd, ditto ditto.
M'Kinlay David, ditto Salt market.
Meikle William, ditto Gallowgate.
Miller Thomas, ditto high ſtreet.
Mitchel Alex. ditto ditto.
Maitland James, taylor, Gallowgate.
M'Alpin Andrew, ditto high ſtreet.
M'Allum Robert, ditto Gallowgate.
M'Allum Duncan, ditto Salt market.
M'Arthur John, ditto King's ſtreet.
M'Kay Robert, ditto Gallowgate.
M'Farlane Orr, ditto ſalt market.
M'Farlane John, ditto Trongate.
M'Farlane Patrick, ditto high ſtreet.
M'Farlane Archibald, ditto King's ſtreet.
M'Ilquham Walter, ditto Trongate.
M'Kechnie James, ditto Gallowgate.
M'Kechnie Lundie, taylor and ſtay maker, ditto.
M'Lachlan John, taylor, Bridgegate.
M'Lean Lachlan, ditto Trongate.
M'Nea Duncan, ditto Gallowgate.
M'Neil Hugh, ditto Salt market.
M'Phail Hector, Gooſe dubs.
M'Rea Peter, ditto Gallowgate.
Miller John, ditto King's ſtreet.
Moncrief John, ditto high ſtreet.
Muir James ditto Salt market.
Marſhall James, ſhoe maker, Gallowgate.
Maxwell John, ditto Trongate.
M'Call J. ſhoe ſhop, Salt market.
M'Crindell John, ditto Argyle ſtreet.
M'Ewan David, ditto Bell's wynd.
M'Millan Daniel, ditto King's ſtreet.

M'Millan Archibald, ſhoe maker, high ſtreet.
M'Farlane Andrew, ditto Stockwell.
M'Kinzie John, ditto Adam's court.
M'Queen James, ditto Blackfriars wynd.
M'Vie John, ditto Salt market.
Miller John, ditto new wynd.
Miller William ditto high ſtreet.
Marſhall and M'Rindel, barbers and hair dreſſers Gibſon's wynd.
Manwell John, ditto Gallowgate.
M'Culloch Samuel, ditto high ſtreet.
M'Aulay James, ditto Gallowgate.
M'Kechnie William, ditto ditto.
M'Kean John, ditto ditto.
M'Indoe John, ditto Stockwell.
Moodie William, ditto Trongate.
Morriſon John ditto Salt market.
Murray Charles, ditto high ſtreet.
Murdoch John, ditto Bell's wyn d
Maxwell Stephen, copper and white iron ſmith, Mawell's ſtreet.
Maxwell, Machen, and Co. founders, ditto.
Miller Robert, copper and white iron ſmith, Salt market.
M'Neil Henry, ditto Stockwell.
Muir John, ditto Bridgegate.
M'Farlane Patrick, watch and clock maker, Gallowgate.
Miller Archibald, ditto ditto.
Mair Peter, ditto Trongate.
M'Cloud William, hammerman, Argyle ſtreet.
M'Culloch Andrew, ditto Stockwell.
M'Gill James, ditto ditto.
M'Gill Ninian, ditto Trongate.
M'Kendrick Daniel, ditto Queen's ſtreet.
M'Carthur John, ditto Salt market.

M'Racht William, hammerman, Argyle ſtreet.
M'Vicar John, ditto Trongate.
Martin James, Vintner, high ſtreet.
Maiklem Finlay, ditto Trongate
Marſhall Robert, ditto old vennel.
M'Alpin Mrs. ditto Trongate.
M'Alpin James, ditto ditto.
M'Adam Walter, ditto and horſe ſetter, Gooſe
  dubs.
M'Coll Duncan, ditto Broom o'law.
M'Donald Malcom, vintner, Trongate.
M'Kinlay Peter, ditto Gallowgate.
M'Farlane Duncan, ditto iron rail, Trongate.
M'Farlane Dougald, ditto Broom o'law.
M'Farlane Donald, ditto Gooſe dubs.
MF'arlane Thomas, ditto Argyle ſtreet.
M'Indoe Hugh, ditto Gallowgate.
M'Indoe James, ditto and ſtabler, Gallowgate.
M'Kean John, ditto King's ſtreet.
M'Fie Duncan, ditto Jamaica ſtreet.
M'Kinzie Samuel, ditto high ſtreet.
M'Lachlan Henry, vintner King's ſtreet.
M'Lean John, ditto Broom o'law.
Miller William, ditto high ſtreet.
Morriſon John, ditto Trongate.
Muir James, ditto Salt market.
Muirhead Robert, ſtabler, new wynd.
M'Nair John, bricklayer, Gallowgate.
M'Water David, brick maker, ditto.
Muir William, tyle maker, calton.
M'Donald Donald, comb maker, Bell's wynd.
M'Indoe James, ditto Gallowgate.
Muir James, ditto Bun's wynd.
M'Aulay Allan, gardner, near Ram's horn
  church.
M'Aulay John, ditto Grahamſton.

Milliken John, reed maker, high ſtreet.
Miller James, ditto ditto.
Menzies and Miller, yarn merchants, ditto.
M'Ewan and Walker, merchants, Gallowgate.
M'Gilchriſt Donald, Salt market foot.
M'Niſh John, ditto Gibſon's land.
M'Leod Malcom, ditto Bridgegate.
M'Leod Alex. ditto ditto.
M'Lean Captain, Salt market foot.
M'Lachlan John, poſt office, Gibſon's wynd.
M'Latchie William, preacher of the Goſpel, high ſtreet.
M'Nair James, cloth lapper, Bell's wynd.
Miller William, keeps a Calender, Gallowgate
Miller Mr. ditto high ſtreet.
M'Allum John, boatman, Broom o'law.
M'Dougald Hugh, ditto ditto.
M'Donald John, ditto ditto.
M'Farlane Peter, ditto toll houſe.
M'Farlane Daniel, ditto Broom o'law.
M'Neil John, ditto ditto.
M'Lelland Hugh, Broom o'law.
Marſhall John in ſhip bank.
Marſhall John, flax dreſſer, Bridgegate.
Maxwell Alex. heel maker, Bridgegate.
M'Aulay John, painter, Trongate.
M'Farlane Parlan, ditto Bridgegate.
M'Farlane Walter, tanner, Gallowgate.
M'Killop Alex. dyer, Bridgegate.
M'Kenrick Robert, maxwell's ſtreet.
M'Lehoſe James, Gallowgate.
M'Laurin Duncan, yarn teller, high ſtreet.
M'Nair James, incle manufacturer, Gallowgate.
M'Neil Neil, armourer, Salt market.
Mitchell Patrick, Stockwell.
Mitchell Peter, rope maker, Bridgegate.

Montgomery James, brewer, Gallowgate.
Montgomery Robert, mason, Qneen's street.
Murray William, shuttle maker, Gallowgate.
Murchie William, cambric dresser, high street.
Miller James, in ship bank.
Murdoch George, porter in ditto.
Munn Archibald, carpenter, Broom o'law.
Mann Duncan, keeper of clerks chamber, high street.
M'Lachlane John, university beadle.
M'Millan Mrs. midwife, Paul's closs, high street.

N

NEilson Walter, merchant, Candlerigs.
 Niven William, ditto high street.
Niven Hugh, lawn and cambric manufacturer.
Newlands Peter, merchant, Salt market.
Neilson John, manufacturer, Gallowgate.
Newlands David, ditto ditto.
Norris Alexander, lawn and cambric manufacturer, high street.
Nicol's Accademy, high street.
Niven William, dealer in china and stone ware, Trongate.
Nisbet and Thomson, woolen and linen drapers, high street.
Nisbet Alex. ditto ditto.
Nisbet Peter, dyer, ditto.
Nisbet John, wright, head of Jamaica street
Napier's auction room Trongate.
Noble Joseph, auctioneer, Trongate.

Napier and Dun, watch and clock makers, head of Stockwell.

Nafmith William, hammerman, Argyle ftreet.

Nicoll John, iron monger, Salt market.

Neilfon John, grocer and ham curer, Salt market.

Neilfon Mrs. grocer and fpirit dealer, King's ftreet.

Neilfon William, rope maker, Jamaica ftreet.

Neilfon William, tallow chandler, Gallowgate.

Neilfon Thomas, flefher, Bridgegate.

Neilfon James, ditto new wynd.

Neilfon William, horfe fetter, Bridgegate.

Napier William, fhoe maker, ditto.

Nicol John, ditto Gallowgate.

Notman James, ditto Bridgegate.

Niven Archibald, boatman, broom o'law.

※※※※※※※※ ※※※※※ ※※※※※※

O

Orr John of Barrowfield, Advocate, one of the City Clerks.

Ofwald George and Co. merchants, Virginia ftreet.

Ofwald James, ditto ditto.

Ofwald Alex. ditto ditto.

Orchart William, woolen and linen draper, Trongate.

Orr Margaret, ditto ditto.

Orr Mrs. bookfeller, Salt market.

Oliphant Francis, ftone ware dealer, King's ftreet.

Ofburn Murray, mathematical inftrument maker, Gallowgate.

Oughterfon Mrs. lets lodgings, Trongate.

P

PAgan John, merchant, high ſtreet.
Patoun Archibald, Trongate.
Paterſon Peter, collector of cuſtoms, Broom
o'law.
Penman John, merchant Gallowgate.
Peters Alex. ditto Adam's court.
Peat James, at Glaſgow tann work Gallowgate.
Pearſton Matthew and John, lawn and cambric
manufacturers, Salt market.
Potts Mr. merchant, Gallowgate.
Paul John, manufacturer, Bun's wynd.
Peacock William, ditto Havanna ſtreet.
Peacock John, ditto new wynd.
Pettigrew Thomas, ditto new vennel.
Paterſon Mrs. feed and nurſery dealer, Trongate.
Paterſon John, ſpirit dealer ditto.
Patoun Andrew, grocer and ſpirit dealer, high
ſtreet.
Patoun David, ditto ditto.
Park Alex. ditto Trongate.
Park William, ditto Stockwell.
Parkhill John, ditto ditto.
Pender John, ditto Gallowgate.
Phillips and Love, grocers and tea dealers, King's
ſtreet.
Phillips Andrew, ditto and ſpirit dealer, ditto.
Pinkerton William, ditto Trongate.
Pollock Allan, ditto and ſpirit and tea dealer,
ditto.

Park Peter, hardware man, Salt market.

Park Thomas, ditto ditto.

Paul Robert and Co. woolen and linen drapers, Gallowgate.

Paterſon Robert, ditto ditto.

Purdie, Crum, and Co. ditto ditto.

Paterſon Thomas, brewer, St Enochs wynd.

Pearſton John, ditto and vintner, Salt market.

Pinkerton William, brewer, Dunlop ſtreet.

Paterſon Archibald, tallow chandler, Gallowgate.

Provan George and Co. dry ſalters, high ſtreet.

Paterſon James, vintner, Trongate.

Paterſon Robert, ditto Argyle ſtreet.

Paterſon John ditto Trongate.

Pearfall John, ditto ditto.

Pettigrew Thomas, ditto ſtockwell.

Pollock James, ditto Trongate.

Pollock Robert, ditto Salt market.

Porteus John, ditto Trongate.

Provan Robert, ditto ditto.

Parker James, baker, King's ſtreet.

Provan Robert, ditto high ſtreet.

Park Alex. barber and hair dreſſer, laigh kirk clofs.

Pollock William, ditto trongate.

Paul John, ſhoe ſhop, Gibſon's wynd.

Paterſon Hugh. ditto King's ſtreet.

Paterſon Andrew, ſhoe maker, trongate.

Paterſon James, ditto high ſtreet.

Paterſon Adam, ditto ditto. •

Paterſon James, wright, Lenox's clofs Bridgegate.

Parkhill James, ditto Bridgegate.

Perry Charles, ditto trongate.

Potter James, ditto ſtockwell.

Purden William, wrights tool maker, high ſtreet.

Paterſon James, cooper, Virginia ſtreet.
Paterſon Archibald, plaiſterer, high ſtreet.
Paterſon James, bruſh maker, Gallowgate.
Pattiſon Benjamin, plummer, Argyle ſtreet
Perry Robert, malt miln maker, ſtockwell.
Paul Mr. gardner, rottenrow.
Peacock Andrew, cutler, Gallowgate.
Phillips Walter, fleſher, King's ſtreet.
Purden William, Hinge maker, Cowcaddens.
Porter John, grieve to Mr Orr of Barrowfield,
    beyond Gallowgate toll.
Poſt Office, middle of Gibſons wynd.

R

Ritchie James and Co. merchants Queen's
    ſtreet.
Ritchie Alex. ditto Horn's land Argyle ſtreet.
Ritchie Henry, ditto Adam's court ditto.
Riddel Henry, ditto Argyle ſtreet.
Robertſon John, caſhier to Cochran, Murdoch
    and Co. Arms Bank, Miller's ſtreet.
Robertſon William, ſmithfield, Broom o'law.
Robertſon John, merchant, foot of King's ſtreet.
Ruſſell David, ditto Gallowgate.
Riddel Alex. ſtamp maker, high ſtreet.
Richardſon James, wool ſhop, ditto.
Riſk William, thread manufacturer and bleacher,
    greenhead.
Reid Thomas, high ſtreet.
Reid Francis, manufacturer, trongate.
Reid and Montgomery, upholſtery ware room,
    ditto.

Renny John, manufacturer, wynd.
Robertfon James, manufacturer, Bun's wynd.
Roger Robert, ditto high ftreet.
Rodger James, lawn and cambric ditto Gallow-
 gate.
Robb David and Co. linen printers, Gallowgate.
Robertfon James and Matthew, printers and book-
 fellers, falt market.
Robertfon Andrew, printer, St Enoch's wynd.
Robertfon John and Co. haberdafhers, trongate.
Roberrfon Lachlan, ftocking fhop, ditto.
Robertfon Robert, hofier, Gallowgate.
Riffo John, makes thermometers barometers, &c.
 at Mr Stirlings, furgeon, falt market.
Reid Mark, grocer and fpirit dealer, high ftreet.
Reid John, ditto ditto.
Robertfon James, ditto ftockwell.
Robertfon Robert, ditto Bridgegate.
Ruffel George, ditto Bell's wynd.
Reid John and Francis, wrights, Candlerigs.
Reid James, ditto Dunlop ftreet.
Robertfon John, ditto Argyle ftreet.
Robertfon John, cooper, Bridgegate.
Robertfon Robert ditto Argyle ftreet.
Roy Walter, cooper, new wynd.
Rankine Charles, painter, ftockwell.
Robertfon and Clow, ditto and oil and colour men,
 trongate.
Reid William, vintner, Gallowgate.
Reid John, ditto trongate.
Robb David, ditto Gallowgate. .
Ruffel George, ditto ditto.
Ronald John, ftabler, Candlerigs.
Rankin Mrs. tobacconift, Bridgegate.
Reid John, ditto high ftreet.
Ralfton William, leather cutter, Gibfon's wynd.

Rankine John, fhoemaker, Bridgegate.
Robertfon Robert, ditto Trongate.
Rofs John, ditto Argyle ftreet.
Rofs Angus, ditto falt market.
Riddel Mrs, Baker and paftry cook, Gibfon's wynd.
Riddel William, Baker, ditto.
Rankine David, barber, high ftreet.
Rankine David junior, ditto and perfumer, Trongate.
Rennie James, ditto Gallowgate.
Reid William, ditto foot of falt market.
Robb David, ditto Gallowgate.
Rankine Mr. taylor, high ftreet.
Ruffel James, ditto Bell's wynd.
Roger Thomas, ftay maker, trongate.
Refton Robert, teller, Thiftle Bank, trongate.
Robertfon James accountant, Merchant bank.
Ruthven John, ftockwell fugar houfe.
Rntherford and Miller, druggifts, high ftreet.
Roger William, comb maker, Gallowgate.
Reid James, plaifterer, high ftreet.
Reid Thomas, trunk maker, falt market.
Rennie David, hammerman, trongate.
Ruffel Thomas, tanner, high ftreet.

S

SCott Robert, merchant, Dunlop ftreet.
Scott Robert, ditto Miller's ftreet.
Scott Thomas, ditto ftockwell.
Scott James, ditto Queen's ftreet.

Scott James, ditto Gallowgate.
Scott Hugh, ditto Adam's court.
Scott Allan, ditto Adam's court.
Scott Allan and Robert, timber merchants.
Shortridge William, merchant, Argyle ſtreet
Shedden John, ditto Adam's court.
Shanks John, ditto high ſtreet.
Sommerville, Gordon, and Co. merchants trongate
Sommerville James, merchant, Miller's ſtreet.
Speirs Alex. and Co. ditto Virginia ſtreet.
Stirling William and Co. whole ſale linen printers
    and merchants, high ſtreet.
Stirling Walter, merchant, Miller's ſtreet.
Stirling, Bell, and Co. ditto Trongate.
Stephenſon and Jamieſon, ditto ditto.
Stephen Alex., agent for great Canal Company,
    Argyle ſtreet.
Steven, Buchanan, and Co. merchants, tron-
    gate.
Sym Andrew, ditto at Gallowgate bridge
Stalker Samuel, accountant, Gallowgate.
Spence Dr Grammar ſchool wynd.
Stenhouse Dr. ſtockwell.
Salmon Peter, manufacturer, Drygate.
Sheddon Thomas and Robert, gauze manufactur-
    ers, high ſtreet.
Sheddon Thomas and Co. lawn and cambric ma-
    nufacturers, ditto.
Smith, Hutchieſon, and Co. whole ſale linen
    drapers, trongate.
Sommervile William and Co. ditto near Bell's
    wynd, high ſtreet.
Shaw William, thread manufacturer, high ſtreet.
Shaw Matthew, ditto ditto.
Simpſon Peter, manufacturer, new wynd.
Simpſon John ditto Caſtlepens land, high ſtreet.

Small William, manufacturer, high ftreet.
Sommerville Walter, ditto high ftreet.
Speedy George, ditto ditto.
Spence Peter, ditto Bun's wynd.
Stirling Archibald, ditto high ftreet.
Stewart Charles, ditto Grammar fchool wynd.
Stark Thomas and Andrew, yarn merchants, high ftreet.
Stenhoufe and Sibbald, ditto high ftreet.
Smellie Archibald, feffion clerk, near foot of falt market.
Smellie Richard, ftocking fhop, trongate.
Smith William, lace and fringe manufacturer, Greenhead.
Shearer Gilbert and Co. woolen drapers, trongate.
Steel William, woolen and linen draper, ditto.
Steven James, ditto high ftreet.
Strang and Stevenfon, ditto King's ftreet.
Stewart Alex. ditto Trongate.
Stewart Robert, ditto Gallowgate.
Stewart Arthur, keeps a callender, Candlerigs
Sharp James, haberdafher, Trongate.
Salmon William, fpirit dealer, Bell's wynd.
Scott James, grocer and ditto near the Crofs falt market.
Scott James ditto Bridgegate.
Scouler James and Co. fpirit dealers, trongate,
Sommerville John, grocer and ditto high ftreet.
Stevenfon Mrs. ditto ditto.
Stewart James, ditto falt market.
Sword John, fpirit dealer, entry to St Andrew's Church, Gallowgate.
Struthers John, brewer and malt man, ditto.
Shaw John and William, Bookfellers, Trongate.

Smith John junior, ditto and circulating library, trongate.

Smith William, printer and bookſeller, ſalt market.

Scott James, copper ſmith and tin plate worker, ditto.

Scott James hammerman wyndhead.

Smith David, edge tool maker, Gallowgate.

Story John, hammerman, ſalt market.

Sutherland Patrick, ditto Bridgegate.

Sawers John, iron monger, Gallowgate.

Sword James, ditto and ſmith, ditto.

Sword Alex. and Benjamin, ditto ditto.

Sword and Blyth, iron founders, butts.

Smith John, watch and clock maker, trongate.

Stewart James, ditto M'Nair's land ditto.

Steven John, ſadler, Gallowgate.

Slofs William, tallow chandler and ſoap maker, Gibſon's wynd.

Stewart Walter, ditto high ſtreet.

Sanderſon William, wright ditto.

Smith Archibald, ditto Candlerigs.

Smith Robert, ditto ditto.

Sommerville George, ditto and inn-keeper, Gallowgate.

Stewart Neil, wright, Kippens clofs high ſtreet.

Stevenſon William, ditto Gallowgate.

Sym James, wright, Bell's wynd.

Smith Peter, ſlater, high ſtr et.

Smith John, ditto ditto.

Shaw William, maſon.

Scouler John, ditto and grocer, Gallowgate

Smellie James, ditto and inn-keeper, Bridgegate.

Sommerville William ditto and ditto high ſtreet.

Scott John, Baker, Gallowgate.

Scott. Gavin, dito ditto.

Scott Thomas, Baker, trongate.
Scott Mrs. ditto ditto.
Smith James ditto falt market.
Smith David, ditto King's ftreet.
Stevenfon David, ditto high ftreet.
Steel William, ditto trongate.
Sheils Andrew, taylor, Gibfon's wynd.
Stirling George, ditto Bell's wynd.
Stewart William, ditto Gallowgate.
Smith Alex. ditto falt market.
Smith Mr. ditto high ftreet.
Salmon James, leather cutter, ditto.
Scott William, fhoe maker, Argyle ftreet.
Scott Robert, ditto Gibfon's wynd.
Semple Robert, ditto high ftreet.
Seth Walter, ditto trongate.
Simpfon James, ditto ditto.
Smith William, ditto falt market.
Short James, ditto ditto.
Stevenfon John, ditto high ftreet.
Steven Archibald, ditto Dunlop ftreet.
Steven Alex. ditto Bridgegate.
Steven and Wilfon, tanners, old vennal
Smith Thomas, ditto new wynd.
Simpfon William, fadler, Charlotte ftreet.
Shearer John fenior, skinner, Bridgegate.
Shearer John junior, ditto ditto.
Shearer John, youngeft, ditto ditto.
Shearer Robert, ditto ditto.
Scott Mrs. vintner, high ftreet.
Scott John, ditto ditto.
Seth James, ditto laigh kirk clofs.
Sheid Mrs. ditto Trongate.
Simpfon Matthew, ditto high ftreet.
Sommerville James, ditto Gallowgate.
Sommerville Walter, ditto ditto.

Speirs William, vintner, King's ſtreet.
Strathern Alex. ditto laigh kirk clofs.
Sym John, ditto trongate.
Stewart William, Gardner, Grammar ſchool wynd.
Sym James, ditto Gallowgate.
Scruton James, teacher of writing, &c. Candle-rigs.
Sellars James, teacher of dancing.
Scott William, tobacconiſt, ſalt market.
Smith James, ditto Gallowgate.
Shaw Archibald, marble cutter, Queen's ſtreet.
Shaw William, at Mr Lindſay's wood yard, Broom o'law.
Shaw William, Adam's court.
Scouler Mrs. Fleſher, new wynd.
Scouler John, ditto ditto.
Scouler James, ditto Bridgegate
Scott James, porter to the Merchant Bank, Max-well's ſtreet.
Semples Miſs, let lodgings, King's ſtreet.
Small, ditto ditto.
Stevenſon John, ditto Bridgegate.
Stevenſon Robert, bruſh maker, Gallowgate.
Stenhonſe Thomas, coach maker, Queen's ſtreet.
Sinclair John, painter, ſtockwell.
Sheriff Clerks office, entry to St Andrew's church, Gallowgate.

T

TAffie John, merchant, Gallowgate.
Tait William, ditto Trongate.
aylor William ditto Gallowgate.

Thomfon and Jack, infurance office, Exchange.

Thomfon Andrew, merchant, Queen's ftreet.

Thomfon Robert, ditto Dunlop ftreet.

Thomfon George, ditto ditto.

Thomfon Robert and Adam, lawn and cambric manufacturers, trongate.

Thomfon Andrew, ditto fhuttle ftreet.

Thomfon and Purdon, linen printers, Trongate.

Thomfon Robert, manufacturer, new vennal.

Thomfon Robert, merchant, trongate.

Todd, Shortridge, and Co. wholefale linen printers, high ftreet.

Todd Cornelius, Goofe dubs.

Trotter John, wholefale linen draper, Bell's wynd.

Thomfon Alex. woolen and linen draper, trongate.

Thomfon James, ditto high ftreet.

Tait Peter, Bookfeller and Printer of the Glafgow Journal, falt market.

Tilloch George and Alex. tobacconifts high ftreet.

Thomfon John, ditto ftockwell.

Tinning Francis, ditto falt market.

Tait James, grocer and fpirit dealer, high ftreet.

Taylor Alex. ditto ditto.

Thomfon Robert and Andrew, grocers and bifcuit bakers, Trongate.

Thomfon James, grocer and fpirit dealer, Gallowgate.

Telfer Thomas, ditto King's ftreet.

Turner John, fpirit dealer, trongate.

Taylor and Hamilton, gold fmiths and jewellers, King's ftreet.

Tait Mrs. fifh hook maker, falt market.

Thomfon Mrs. copper and white iron fmith, high ftreet.

Thomfon Alex. hammerman, Grammar fchool
wynd.

Turner Archibald, iron monger, near head of
falt market.

Taffie John, Glove fhop, King's ftreet.

Taffie William, ditto foot of falt market.

Thomfon John, fadler, falt market.

Thomfon William, ditto Gallowgate.

Tait Mrs, vintner, ditto.

Towart William, ditto Howgate.

Tennent John and Robert, Brewers and Maltmen
Drygate.

Todd James, Maltman, Gallowgate.

Taylor John, leather cutter, high ftreet.

Taylor John, fhoe maker, Bridgegate.

Telfer William, fhoe fhop, Gibfon's wynd.

Tarbet David, taylor, high ftreet.

Taylor Neil, ditto high ftreet.

Telfer William, mafon, Havanna ftreet.

Telfer William, hofier, Gallowgate.

Thomfon Richard, Baker, King's ftreet.

Thomfon Thomas, dyer, fpout mouth.

Townend William, tallow chandler, Bell's wynd.

Trueman Willlam, Rope work ftockwell

Turner Andrew, boatman, Broom o'law.

Turnbull John, hofier, high ftreet.

Turnbull, Thomas, wheel wright, high ftreet.

Turnbull William, horfe fetter, falt market.

Town Hofpital and Infirmary, Clyde ftreet.

U

URE and M'Gilchrift, woolen and linen dra-
pers, high ftreet.
Ure John, ditto Gallowgate.
Ure John, merchant, high ftreet.
Ure Andrew, yarn merchant, ditto.
Ure and Galbraith, hard ware men, falt market.
Ure Alex. mafon, King's ftreet.
Ure Walter, fhoe maker, new wynd.
Ure John, grocer, Gallowgate.
Ure John, Baker, Bridgegate.
Ure James, ditto ditto.
Ure John, ditto ftockwell.
Ure Robert, barber, falt market.
Urie William, cooper, ftockwell.
Urie Matthew, cooper, ditto.
Vance John, leather cutter, Gibfon's wynd
Vaffie Robert, cordner, high ftreet.
Veitch Alex. Trongate.

W

WArdrop James and John, merchants, high
ftreet.
Wardlaw William, ditto Charlotte ftreet.
Wallace John, linen and woolen draper Gallowgate.
Warrand John, yarn merchant and linen draper,
Gibfon's clofs.

Warrand Alex. merchant, falt market.
Wilfon, Cumberland, and Co. ditto Argyle ftreet
Wilfon Alex. and Sons, proprietors of the letter foundery, high ftreet.
Wilfon William, merchant, ftockwell.
Wilfon William, accountant, Dunlop ftreet.
Wilfon John, writer, one of the city clerks, Gal-lowgate.
Whytelaw and Simpfon, fadlers, high ftreet.
Whytelaw James, Charlotte ftreet.
Whytelaw Thomas, merchant falt market.
Whyte Robert, woolen and linen draper, high ftreet.
Watfon E. haberdafher, trongate.
Walker Alex. manufacturer, ditto.
Wales William, ditto new vennal.
Watfon John, ditto ftockwell.
Watfon John, ditto Havanna ftreet.
Watfon William, ditto ditto.
Whyte William, thread ditto high ftreet.   .
White Robert, manufacturer, Havanna ftreet.
White Robert, ditto new vennal.
White John, ditto Grammar fchool wynd,
Weir Andrew, ditto Havanna-ftreet.
Wilfon and Clark, filk ditto Anderftown.
Wilfon John, manufacturer, Gallowgate.
Wifon John, ditto old vennal.
White and Gibfon, iron mongers, falt market.
Wilfon John, ditto Trongate.
Wright Robert, hard ware man, falt market.
Wright James, jeweller, King's ftreet.
Wright John, junior, merchant, Trongate.
Wright John, auctioneer, ditto.
Williamfon John, bookfeller, falt merket. .
Walker George, grocer and fpirit dealer, Gallow-gate.
Wiflon Archibald, ditto Trongate.

Wright John, grocer and ſpirit dealer, Argyle ſtreet.

Wright Archibald, Druggiſt, Trongate.

Wilſon Walter, feed and nurſery man, ditto.

Waddel William, tobacconiſt, Gallowgate.

Watt Mrs. ditto ditto.

Walker James, Baker, high ſtreet.

Warnock Andrew, ditto St Enochs wynd.

Weir James, ditto high ſtreet.

White Andrew, ditto Trongate.

White Alex. ditto Reids land high ſtreet.

Wright-John, ditto Trongate.

Wright John, ditto Bridgegate.

Waterſton John, leather ſhop, Trongate.

Waddel John, ditto Gallowgate.

Wardrop John, cordner, ſalt market.

Weſt Thomas, ditto Bridgegate.

Weir John, ditto ſalt market.

Williamſon Gavin, ditto high ſtreet.

Wilſon John, ditto Grammar ſchool wynd.

Wright Daniel, turner, new wynd.

Waddel Robert, wright, ſalt market.

Wardrop John, ditto Argyle ſtreet.

Wilſon John, ditto Gallowgate

Wright John, ditto ditto.

Wylie James, ditto ditto.

Wilkie James, wheel wright.

Wardrop Daniel, maſon, Argyle ſtreet.

Wilſon Thomas, ditto ſalt market.

Watt Mrs. vintner, ditto.

Wardrop James, ditto high ſtreet.

Winning Robert, ditto Bell's wynd.

Wilſon David, ditto Gallowgate.

Wilſon George ditto Trongate.

Wood James, ditto King's ſtreet.

Watſon Gabriel, Edinburgh carrier, Gallowgate.

Watfon William, clerk to the New Caſtle waggon, WGallowgate.

alker William, teller in the Glaſgow Arms WBank.

Wyllie Broadie, accountant in ditto.

Wardrop William, ſhip Bank.

Watfon Robert, teacher of dancing, ſalt market.

Wright John, teacher of Engliſh, high ſtreet.

Weir Walter, cooper, Gallowgate.

White David, ditto Bridgegate.

White Peter, ditto ſalt market.

Williamſon Peter, ditto ſtockwell.

Watfon William, Fleſher, Bridgegate

Watfon Thomas, ditto back wynd.

Wingate Thomas, tallow chandler, high ſtreet.

Wyllie and M'Allum, ditto King's ſtreet.

Wright Lanchlan, confectioner, back wynd.

Wallace Mrs. makes burying crapes, Trongate.

Wallace Robert, painter, high ſtreet.

Whytelaw John, barber, Maxwell's ſtreet.

Wharton Robert, ditto Bridgegate.

Wilfon William, ditto ſtockwell.

Wotherfpoon Richard, ditto King's ſtreet.

Watfon Archibald, hammerman, Gallowgate.

Watt James, ditto high ſtreet.

Wright Malcom, wire worker, Trongate.

Wilfon James, gardner, Queen's ſtreet.

Wyllie Mrs. lets lodgings, Trongate.

Watfon, Mr. ſtay maker, Gallowgate.

Watt James, Taylor, ditto.

Wright J. ſtay maker, Trongate.

Walker William, hoſier, Grammar ſchool wynd.

Walker Robert, boatman, Broom o'law.

Wright Peter, tide officer, Bridgegate.

Y

YOung John, merchant, Argyle ſtreet.
Young David, ſilk mercer and haberdaſher, Trongate.
Yonng James, merchant, Gallowgate.
Young John, auctioneer, high ſtreet.
Young John and Son, woolen and linen drapers, ditto.
Younger George, Gibſon's land.
Young William, Delft houſe.
Young Mr. teacher of Engliſh, high ſtreet.
Young John, cooper, Candlerigs.
Young Robert, ditto ditto.
Younger Andrew, barber, Gallowgate.
Young Hugh, grocer, high ſtreet.
Young John, wright, Bell's wynd.
Young James, ditto high ſtreet.
Young Thomas, Greenock and Edinburgh carrier, Bell's wynd.
Young David, glover, Bridgegate.
Young Peter, diito ditto.
Young William, dyer, Havannah ſtreet.
Young Hugh, ſtabler, high ſtreet.

Z

ZUill David, woolen and linen draper, trongate.
Zuill Thomas, ſtockwell.
Zuill James, Baker, high ſtreet.

An Alphabetical Table of the Arrival and Departures of the differeut Posts at and from the Post office of Glasgow.

S U N D A Y.
Arrivals.
Eight morning,
Aras,
Bonnaw,
Bo-nefs,
Bowmore,
Campbelton,
Dumbarton
Edinburgh
Falkirk
Fort William
Inverary
Ireland
Kilfyth
Linlithgow
Oban.
Portnacroifh
Strontian
Tarbet.
  Five afternoon,
Greenock
Port-Glafgow.
  Eight at night.
Beith, Hamilton
Paifley
  Departures.
Eight morning
Paifley
  Ten forenoon,
Aras, Bonnaw,
Bowmore
Campbelton
Dumbarton
Douglafs
Fort William
Hamilton
Inverary, Lanark
Oban
Portnacroifh
Strontian, Tarbet
  Twelve noon,
Ayr, Ballantrea
Girvan, Irvine

Ireland
Kilmarnock
Maybole
Neilfton
Stewartton
  Two afternoon,
Greenock
Port-Glafgow
Rothfay
  Nine at night,
Bo-nefs
Edinburgh
Falkirk, Kilfyth
Linlithgow

M O N D A Y
  Arrivals,
Five afternoon,
Ayr, Ballantrea
Girvan, Greenock
Ireland, Irvine
Kilmarnock
Maybole, Neilfton
Port-glafgow
Rothfay
Stewarton
Stranrawer
  Early morning,
Carlifle, Cumnock
Dumfries
Kilmarnock
London
Sanquhar
Thornhill
All the Weft of
  England.
  Departures.
Nine at night,
Alloa, Bo-nefs
Crieff
Edinburgh, &c.
Falkirk, Kilfyth
Linlithgow
Stirling
  Eleven forenoon,

Edinburgh, &c. per
  Exprefs
  Twelve noon,
Cumnock
Carlifle, Dumfries
Ireland
Kilmarnoc k
Sanquhar
Thornhiil
All the Weft of
  England
  Eight morning
Paifley
  Two afternoon
Greenock
Port Glafgow.

T U E S D A Y.
  Arrivals,
  Eight morning,
Alloa, Aras
Bonnaw, Bo-nefs
Bowmore
Campbelton
Crieff
Dumbarton
Edinburgh, &c.
Falkirk
Fort William
Inverary, Kilfyth
Linlithgow, Oban
Portnacroifh
Stirling, Strontian
Tarbet
  Five at night
Greenock
Port-Glafgow
  Eight at night
Beith, Hamilton
Paifley
  Departures,
  Ten forenoon,
Aras, Bowmore
Bonnaw
Campbelton

Dumbarton
Fort. William
Inverary, Oban
Portnacroifh
Strontian, Tarbet
   Twelve noon
Ayr, Ballantrea
Girvan, Ireland
Kilmarnock
Maybole Neilfton
Stewarton
Stranrawer
   Nine at night,
Alloa, Bo-nefs
Crieff
Edinburgh, &c.
Falkirk, Kilfyth
Linlithgow
Stirling
   Eight morning,
Paifley
   Ten forenoon,
Hamilton
   Two afternoon,
Greenock
Port Glafgow
Rothfay

WEDNESDAY

ARRIVALS.

   Very early,
Carlifle, Cumnock
Dumfries
Ireland
Kilmarnock
Sanquhar
Thornhill
Weft of England
   Eight morning,
Alloa, Bo-nefs
Crieff, Dumbarton
Edinburgh, &c.
Falkirk, Kilfyth
Linlithgow
Stirling

   Five afternoon,
Ayr, Ballantrae
Greenock, Girvan
Ireland, (two arriv.)
Irvine
Maybole, Neilfton
Port Glafgow
Rothfay
Stewarton
Stranrawer
   Eight night
Hamilton, Lanark
Paifley

DEPARTURES.

   Nine Night
Alloa-Bo-nefs
Crieff
Edinburgh, &c.
Falkirk, Kilfyth
Linlithgow
   Eight morning,
Paifley
   Ten forenoon,
Dumbarton
Hamilton, Lanark,
   Twelve noon,
Ayr, Irvine
Kilmarnock
Neilfton
   Two afternoon,
Greenock
Port Glafgow

THURSDAY.

ARRIVALS.

   Eight morning
Alloa, Aras
Bonaw, Bo-nefs
Bowmore
Campbeltown
Crieff, Dumbarton
Edinburgh, &c.
Falkirk
Fort William

Inverary, Kilfyth
Linlithgow
Portnacroifh
Strontian, Stirling
Tarbet
   Five afternoon,
Ayr, Greenock
Girven, Irvine
Kilmarnock
Maybole, Neilfton
Port Glafgow
Stewarton
   Eight at night
Beith, Hamilton
Paifley

DEPARTURES.

   Ten morning,
Aras, Bonnaw
Bowmore
Campbelton
Dumbarton
Fort William
Inverary, Oban
Portnacroifh
Strontian, Tarbet
   Ten forenoon,
Hamilton
   Twelve noon,
Cumnock, Carlifle
Dumfries
Ireland, Irvine
Kilmarnock
Sanquhar
Stewarton
Strontian
Thornhill
Weft of England
   Two afternoon,
Greenock
Port Glafgow
Rothfay
   Nine at night
Alloa Bo-nefs
Crieff
Edinburgh, &c.
Falkirk, Kilfyth

K

Linlithgow
Stirling
  Eight morning,
Paifley

FRIDAY.

ARRIVALS.

Eight morning,
Alloa
Bo-nefs
Crieff
Dumbarton
Edinburgh
Falkirk
Linlithgow
Stirling
  Five afternoon,
Ayr
Ballantrea
Greenock
Girven
Irvine
Kilmarnock
Maybole
Neilfton
Port Glafgow
Rothfay
Stewarton
  Eight night,
Hamilton
Lanark, Paifley

DEPARTURES.

Nine night,
Alloa, Bo-nefs
Crieff, Edinburgh
Falkirk, Linlithgow
  Twelve noon,
Ayr, Ballantrea
Girven, Ireland
Irvine, Kilmarnock
Maybole, Neilfton
Stewarton
Stranrawer
  Two afternoon,
Greenock
Port Glafgow
  Eight morning,
Paifley, Stirling

SATURDAY.

ARRIVALS.

Early morning,
Cumnock, Carlifle
Dumfries, Ireland
Kilmarnock
Sanquhar, Thornhill
Weft of England
  Eight morning,
Alloa, Bo-nefs
Crieff, Dumbarton
Edinburgh, &c.
Falkirk, Kilfyth

Linlithgow
Stirling
  Five afternoon
Ayr, Ballantrea
Ireland
Irvine
Girven, Greenock
Kilmarnock
Maybole, Neilfton
Port Glafgow
Stewarton
Stranra wer
  Eight night
Paifley

DEPARTURES.

Eight night,
Carlifle, Cumnock
Dumfries
Kilmarnock
London, Sanquhar
Thornhill
  Twelve noon,
Ayr, Irvine
Kilmarnock
Neilfton
Stewarton
  Two afternoon,
Greenock
Port Glafgow
  Ten forenoon
Hamilton
  Eight morning
Paifley

Arrival and Dpartures of FOREIGN MAILS.

ARRIVALS.

Wednef. & Saturday.

France
Flanders
Holland
Germany

Poland
Ruffia
Spain
Sweden
Denmark
Portugal, as the
  Packet arrives.

DEPARTURES.

Sunday & Thurfday

France
Flanders
Holland

Germany	Spain	Portugal,	Thurſday
Poland	Sweden	only	
Ruſſia	Denmark		

N. B. A mail is diſpatched to North America, and the Weſt Indies on the Friday before the firſt Wedneſday of every month.

POSTAGE for a ſingle letter to any of the following places, and ſo in proportion for double, triple, &c.

	ſh.	d.						
			Holland	o	8	Portugal	2	2
Azores or			Geneva	o	8	Ruſſia	1	8
the Weſt-	2	2	Germany	1	8	Sweden	1	8
ern Iſlands			Italy	1	11	Switzerland		
Denmark	1	8	Madeira	2	2	(except Ge-	1	11
France	o	8	Minorca	1	11	neva.)		
Flanders	o	8	Poland	1	8	Spain	2	2

Departure to the following towns by Carliſle, on Monday, Thurſday and Saturday.

Appleby	Keſwick	Richmond
Barnard Caſtle	Lancaſter	Stafford
Bedall	Liverpool	Stratford
Birmingham	Mancheſter	Stone
Bolton	Middlewich	Warrington
Brough	Namptwitch	Warwick
Carliſle	Northwich	Walſel
Cockermouth	Ormſkirk	Whitehaven
Coventry	Penrith	Wiggan
Henly in Arden	Preſton	Woolverhampton
Kendal	Preſcot	Workington

CARRIERS QUARTERS.

From whence.	Where Lodged	Arri.	Dep.
Alloa		Wed.	Wed.
Aberdeen	Ronald's Candlerigs	uncer	uncer
Ardrie	Loudon's Gallowgate	Mon.	Mon
Auchterarder	Brown's Black F. wynd	u n c	Wed
Bochlivy	Ures High-ſtree	Tueſ.	Thu

Bathgate	Loudon's Gailowgate. (fortnightly)	Wed.	Wed.
Beith	M'Alpin's Trongate	Tuef.	Wed.
Ditto	Neilfon's N wynd	Tuef.	Thur
Buchanan	Williamfon's ditto	Wed.	uncer
Bonnaw	Giles's Trongate	uncer	Frid.
Cumnock	M'Indoe's Gallowgate	Thur	Thur
Callander	Moor's Salt market (fortnightly)	Wed.	Wed.
Carluke	Somerville's Gallowgate	Tuef.	uncer
Crieff	Arthur's High ftreet	uncer	Satur
Carlifle	Fi dlay's Trongate	Frid.	Wed.
Ditto	Ditto ditto	Mon.	Thur
Dundee		Wed,	Frid.
Dumfries	M'Indoe's Gallowgate	Thur	Thur
Dumfermline	Ronald's Trongate (fotnightly)	Wed.	Wed.
Dumbarton	Buchanan's Argyle's-ftreet	Tuef	Satur
Ditto	Ditto ditto	Frid.	nncer
Dunkeld	Findlay's Trongate	uncer	Thur
Drummond	Williamfon's N. wynd	Wed.	Thuf
Edinburgh	Watfon's Gallowgate	Satur	Wed.
Ditto	Ditto ditto	Tuef.	Tuef.
Ditto	Bell's Candlerigs	Satur	Wed.
Fintry	Gile's Trongate	Tuef.	Wed.
Falkirk	Ronald's Candlerigs	Wed	Wed.
Ditto	Gile's Trongate	Wed	Wed.
Gartmore	Craig's O. wynd	uncer	uncer
Greenock	Young's Bell's wynd	Wed.	Mon.
Ditto	Auld's Gallowgate	Wed.	Mon.
Hamilton	Somerville's ditto	Wed.	Wed.
Ditto	Watfon's ditto	Mon.	Mon.
Inverary	Buchanan's Argyle-ftreet	uncer	uncer
Irvine	Ronald's Candlerigs	Tuef.	Wed.
Kilfyth	Arthur's High.ftreet	Wed.	Wed.
Kilwinning	Ronald's Candlerigs	Wed.	Wed.
Kilbarchan	Smellie's Bridegate	Wed.	Wed.
Kilmarnock	Gile's Trongate	Wed.	Wed.
Ditto		Frid.	Frid.
Kirkintulloch	Marfhall's High-ftreet	Wed.	Wed.
Kippen	Ure's High ftreet	Tuef.	Wed.
Lanark	Gib's Gallowgate	Tuef.	Wed.
Linlithgow	Gile's Trongate	Tuef	Wed.
Machlin		Wed	Thur
Newcaftle	Watfon's Gallowgate	Frid.	Satur
Newmills	Borland N. wynd	Tuef	Wed.
Perth	Ronald's Candlerigs	Wed.	Wed.
Paifley	Findlay's Trongate	daily	daily
Stirling		Wed.	Wed.
St Ninians	Giles ditto	Wed.	Wed.

Strathven	M'Indoe's Gallowgate	Tuef.	Wed.
Saltcoats	Ronald's Candlerigs	Tuef.	Wed.
Stewarton	Ronald's ditto	Tuef.	Wed.
Thornhill	Ure's High ſtreet	Tuef.	Wed.

STAGE COACHES.

'Twixt EDINBURGH and GLASGOW.

Three Machines ſet out from each place every day, at eight morning, they ſtop on the road and change horſes. Tickets, 10s. 6d. each. ſold by J. Buchanan and A Dumbar, Glaſgow, and by Geo. Warden, and John Cameron, Graſs-markct Edinburgh---- Another from Mr Dick's, Glaſgow, every Monday, Wedneſday, and Friday, and from Mrs Montgomery's Graſs-market Edin. every Tueſday, Thurſday, and Saturday, at ſame hour, Tickets 8s. 6d. And one from Patrick Heron's Glaſgow, and Robertſons Pleaſance, Edinburgh every day. Tickets 10 s. 6d.

DUMBARTON DILIGENCE,

Sets out from Duries every day of the week in Summer, and on Monday, Wedneſday, and Friday in Winter.

PAISLEY DILIGENCE,

Sets out from Pinkcrtons and Dunbars, Trongate, twice every day but Sabbath.

GREENOCK DILIGENCE.

Sets out every day of the week, from Somervilles, Gallowgate, and Dumbars, Trongate

KILMARNOCK DILIGENCE,

Sets out from Reids Gallowgate, every Monday and Thurſday.

CARLISLE DILIGENCE,

Sets out every lawful day from Buchanans, Gallowgate.

HAMILTON DILIGENCE,

Sets out fram M'Indoes, Gallowgate, every Monday, Wedneſday and Saturday.

AYR DILIGENCE,

Sets out every Thurſday and Friday from Buchanans, Gallowgate.

STIRLING DILIGENCE,

Sets out every Tueſday and Thurſday, from Wilſons Gallowgate.

This publication having been delayed fomewhat beyond the time expected, arifing from unexpected and unforefeen difficulties, (it being the firft of the kind attempted in this place), and from a defire of having it as complete and correct as poffible. The Publifher hopes the Candid and Generous Public, and his numerous Subfcribers, will excufe him.

Notwithftanding his diligence to have all the people concerned in bufinefs inferted, he may have omitted or mifnamed fome of them ; to make all the amends he can, he will, as far as lies in his power, in the fupplement he intends to publifh about the month of Auguft, rectify any miftakes, and infert thefe who have been omitted. For which purpofe he earneftly requefts the Gentlemen, &c. who may find themfelves omitted, to fend their names and places of abode to his ftationary fhop a little above the Crofs, and they fhall be properly inferted.

A LIST of the MERCHANTS, &c. of the Town of Paisley, 1783.

A

ALexander James, manufacturer, causeyside.
Allan John, merchant, Snedon street.
Andrew Matthew, manufacturer, Causeyside.
Anderson John, ditto Orchard street.
Alexander Robert Fulton thread ditto bridge str.
Angelie William, dyer, St marions wynd.
Anderson William, hutt.
Alason John, baker, high street.

B

Barr Robert, manufacturer, gause St. Newtown
Barr James, ditto Causeyside street.
Barbour John, thread ditto maxweltoun.
Barbour John, junior, merchant, ditto.
Barclay Francis, thread manufacturer, James's str.
Barclay Robert, manufacturer, Causeyside.
Barrie Thomas, tobacconist, high street.
Barrie Andrew, grocer, ditto.
Bell and Maxwell, hard and soft soap boilers, Sawcell.
Bennet Robert, grocer cross.
Bennet and Co. Messrs, silk manufacturers, silk street new town.

Birkmyre George, thread manufacturer high ſtreet.
Bisland Alex. wright, high ſtreet
Bisland Thomas, wood merchant, ditto.
Biggar Robert, thread manufacturer, Cauſeyſide.
Blair James, writer, Gauze ſtreet new town.
Blackwood Robert, vintner, ſilk ſtreet ditto.
Black John, thread manufacturer, Snedon.
Bowman John, leather merchant, bridgend.
Bowie Henry, manufacturer, Gordon's lone.
Browning Gavin, druggiſt, crofs.
Brown Robert thread manufacturer, Snedon
Brown and Sharp Meſſrs. manufacturers, new
    ſtreet.
Brown Thomas, brewer, Crafthead.
Brown Matthew, ditto ditto
Brodie Robert, grocer, ſand holes.
Braid Robert, fleſher, moſſrow.
Buchanan Herbert and Co. merchants, gauze ſtr.
    new town.
Buchanan William, merchant Snedon.
Buchanan James, ditto high ſtreet.
Buchanan Robert, manufacturer, gauze Str. new
    town.
Buchanan Archibald, calligo printer, nether com-
    mon.

C

CArlyſle William, Thread manufacturer, Sne-
  don.
Carlyle James and Co. manufacturers, Snedon.
Caldwell John, thread ditto ditto.
Caldwell Thomas, merchant, Cauſeſide.
Caldwell George, bookſeller, Moſs row.
Carſon and Hunter, timber merchants, Snedon.

Carſwell Robert, cooper, moſs row.
Campbell Archibald, manufacturer, Cauſeyſide.
Campbell William and Thomas, tanners, St mari-
on's wynd.
Campbell William, Feſher, St Marions ſtreet.
Campbell James, ditto Moſs row.
Chriſtie, Carſe, and Co. timber merchants, Craft
head.
Chriſtie John, ditto Gauſe ſtreet new town
Chambers James, grocer, Snedon.
Clark John, ſilk liſh maker, ditto.
Clark James, hedle twine maker, Cotton ſtreet
new town.
Clark Robert, ſhoe maker, Croſs.
Cochran John, yarn merchant, high ſtreet.
Cochran John, junior, merchant, Snedon.
Cochran John, manufacturer new ſtreet.
Cochran James, merchant, Snedon.
Cochran John, dyer, Sawcell.
Crawford John, merchant, high ſtreet.
Crawford John, vintner, Snedon
Craig James, leather merchant, high ſtreet.
Croſs Robert, merchant, Greenlaw.
Croſs Walter, manufacturer, Cauſeyſide.
Crow and Duncan Meſſrs, ſmiths, Cauſeyſide.

D

Dalgliſh John, broker, croſs.
Davis Robert, grocer, high ſtreet.
Denniſton Robert, bleacher, Snedon.
Dick Robert, manufacturer, Caſyſide.
Dick Robert, hedle twine maker, Maxwelton.
Dowie David, grocer and ſeeds man, high ſtreet.
Dun Andrew, merchant, high ſtreet.
Dun Mrs. vintner, Bridgend.
Dun Alex. glover, ditto.

E

E Afton David, baker, Crofs.
Edmifton, Lothian, and Co. ditto new town.
Ellis, filk manufacturer, Snedon.
Elliot and Dibbs, filk manufacturers, wood
fide.

F

F Indlay John, Minifter High Church, Snedon.
Ferrier, Pollock, and Co. filk manufacturers,
Crofs.
Fergufon John Stay maker, ditto.
Findlay John, Smith and Ferrier, high ftreet.
Flint William, grocer, Gauze ftreet new town.
Fouler John, ditto ditto.
Fulton Meffrs, filk manufacturers Maxweltons.
Fulton Hugh, feed merchant, Crofs.
Fulton Hugh, Surgeon, ditto.
Fulton David, Taylor, ditto.

G

G Illies Colin, Minifter, Laigh Church Snedon.
Gardiner Archibald, thread manufacturer, new
ftreet,

Gardener John, merchant, high ſtreet.
Galbreath John, Smith and Ferrier Moſs row.
Gentles John, Baker, Gauze ſtreet new town.
Gerard James, Spirit dealer, Bridgend.
Gibſon Alex. writer, Townhead.
Gibſon James, ditto high ſtreet.
Gibſon William, Surgeon, Croſs.
Gibb James, ſilk manufacturer, Bridge ſtreet.
Gibb John, vintner, high ſtreet.
Gilmour Patrick, manufacturer, Orchard ſtreet.
Gilmour James, merchant, ditto.
Gillies Malcolm, Silver ſmith, high ſtreet.
Gilroy Charles, Baker, Croſs.
Grahame Mrs. vintner, high ſtreet.
Grahame Rodger, Soap boyler, Snedon.
Grahame James, Cooper, Cauſeyſide.

H

Hart James and Son, manufacturers, Caſyſide.
    Harriſon Joſeph and Co. tanners Snedon.
Hannah John, vintner, new ſtreet.
Hall John, grocer, Gauze ſtreet new town.
Hendry and Robertſon, ſilk manufacturers, ditto.
Hepburn and Watt, ditto ditto.
Heghet John, grocer, Cotton ſtreet new town.
Hill Ninian, keeps a Calender, Bridgend.
Holmes Joſeph and Co. ſilk manufacturers, Town head.
Hunter Robert, merchant, high ſtreet.
Hume William, Engineer, Abbey cloſs.

✕✕✕✕✕✕✕✕✕✕✕✕✕✕✕✕

J

JAmiefon Hugh, manufacturer, Orchard ftreet.
Jamiefon Robert, ditto Caufeyfide
Jamefon and Co. Cotton manufacturers, Abbey
ftreet.
Jamiefon William, merchant, Crofs.
Jamiefon William, ditto Smithills.

✕✕✕✕✕✕✕✕✕✕✕✕✕✕✕✕

K

KER Thomas, Poft mafter, Mofs row.
Ker Thomas, writer, Smith hills.
Ker Thomas, Baker, high ftreet.
Ker Daniel, mealdealer, ditto.
Ker Andrew, wright, Snedon.
Kibble James, writer, Smith hills.
Kibble Thomas, ditto Crofs.
King William, Dyer, Dyers wynd.
King John, Rope maker, high ftreet.
King David, Plaifterer, Silk ftreet new town.
Knox John, yarn merchant, high ftreet.

✕✕✕✕✕✕✕✕✕✕✕✕✕✕✕

L

LOwndes James and Co. filk manufacturers,
Snedon.
Love John, ditto new ftreet.
Love James filk manufacturer, abbey bridge ftre e

Lochead Matthew, manufacturer, Causeyside.
Lochead Robert, vintner, town head.
Lochead Walter, Baker, high street.
Lochead John, Meal dealer, Calton.
Liper Andrew, Barber, St marions wynd.

M

Maxwell Charles, timber merchant, Mofs row.
Maxwell and Patrick, thread manufacturers Snedon.
Marshall Thomas, ditto Causeyside
Mann Alex. wright. wellmeadow.
Main Peter, thread manufacturer Causeyside.
M'Errol John, silk ditto Maxwelton.
M'Arthur Peter, Bookseller, Crofs.
M'Gowan Matthew. merchant, ditto.
M'Grigor Duncan, Gauze street new town.
M'Kechney Alex. shuttle maker, James street.
M'Kechney William, Victualer, Mofs row.
M'Korkindale David, flesher, ditto.
M'Lellan John, heddle maker, hut.
M'Lellan John, junior, silk lish maker, well-
  meadow.
M'Lean John, manufacturer, Orchard street.
M'Lean David, ditto ditto.
M'Murchie Niel, Causeyside.
M·Nair Alex. merchant, high street.
Montgomery Matthew, thread manufacturer, Mofs
  row.
Moody Matthew and Son, ditto town head.
Morrison James, merchant, Crofs.
Miller James, soap and candle maker, high street.
Mure William, Maltman, high street.
  ure John, carrier to Glafgow, St Marions wynd.

N

NEilſon and Hunter, manufacturers, Cauſeyſide.

Neilſon William, ditto ditto.

Neilſon John, grocer, Croſs.

Neilſon Walter, vintner, James ſtreet.

Niven, Stevenſon, and Pagan, ſilk manufacturers, high ſtreet.

Niſbet William, meſſenger, high ſtreet.

O

ORR, Craig, and Stow, Great George ſtreet.
Orr William and Sons, Cauſeyſide.

Orr Robert, ſenior, manufacturer, Cauſeyſide.

Orr Robert, junior, ditto ditto.

Orr William and John, merchants, Gauze ſtreet new town.

Orr William, manufacturer, Orchard ſtreet.

Orr James, writer, Bridgend.

Orr and Kibble, Smith hills.

P

PAiſley James, merchant, Croſs.
Patiſon John, manufacturer, town head.

Patiſon John, junior, ditto Croſs.

Patifon William, wright and glazier, town head
Patton James, grocer, fandholes.
Park Robert, thread manufacturer, Smith hills.
Pollock George, ftamp mafter, Gauze ftreet
   new town.
Pollock Alex, filk li fh maker, maxwelton.
Purdie Andrew, wright, Snedon.

***

R

Ramfay, William, manufacturer, Caufeyfide.
   Ramfay Thomas, Baker high ftreet.
Ralfton Alex. Flefher, St Marions wynd.
Renfrew John, manufacturer, Caufeyfide.
Reid Fulton, grocer, fandholes.
Ritchardfon John, Smith, Gauze ftreet new town
Robertfon John, thread manufacturer, Caufey-
   fide.
Robertfon Robert, ditto ditto.
Robertfon John, grocer, fandholes.
Robertfon William, merchant, Snedon.
Rofs Charles, Greenlaw.
Rule James, baker, Caufeyfide.

***

S

Snodgrafs John, Minifter, New Church.
Sempill William, Gauze dreffer, Gordons lone
Simpfon Claud, writer, high ftreet.

Simpſon James, Surgeon Crofs.
Sim Peter, hardware merchant, ditto.
Sinclair James, wright, moſsrow.
Smith John, junior, manufacturer Orchard
 ſtreet.
Smith and Grahame ditto high ſtreet.
Smith John, meal dealer, Cauſeyſide·
Smith Andrew, manufacturer, ditto.
Spier Robert, tobacconiſt, high ſtreet
Spier John, Fleſher, mofs row.
Stewart John, manufacturer, Orchard ſtreet.
Stewart William, Surgeon, high ſtreet.
Stewart and Orr, town head.
Stewart William linen draper & haberdaſher Crofs
Stewart John, grocer, ditto.
Stevenſon John and Son, merchants, ditto
Stevenſon William, ſilk manufacturer, new ſtreet.
Stirling William, manufacturer, Gordon s lone.
Stirling James and Co. hardware merchants, Crofs
Stirling John, ſaddler, high ſtreet.
Steel James, manufacturer, Cafyſide.
Storie John, merchant, ditto.

T

Tarbet John, thread manufacturer Cauſeyſide.
 Tarbet James, ditto maxwelton.
Taylor Alex. Surgeon, mofs row.
Thomſon James, tobacconiſt, Crofs.
Train John, merchant, high ſtreet.
Twige William, ſilk manufacturer, bridgend

W

Walkingſhaw Hugh, manufacturer, cauſey-
ſide.
Walkingſhaw Robert and John, ditto ditto.
Walkinſhaw James, writer, high ſtreet.
Walkinſhaw Robert, ditto bridgend.
Wallace William and John, ſilk manrs. Snedon
Walker Samuel. thread ditto ditto.
Warnock John, grocer, croſs
Waterſton James, Painter, ditto.
Watt William, baker, high ſtreet.
Weir Walter, manufacturer, cauſeyſide.
Weir Alex. merchant, Croſs
Weir John bookſeller, ditto.
White Robert, manr. cotton ſtreet new town.
White John, ſurgeon, high ſtreet.
White Andrew, hardware man, ditto
White Andrew, ſhoe maker, croſs.
White James, heddle maker, ſnedon.
Whitehead Thomas, tanner, ſeedhills,
Whytehill John merchant, high ſtreet.
Wilſon John, manufacturer, town head.
Wilſon Hugh, yarn merchant, bridgend.
Wilſon James, merchant, croſs.
Wilſon James, writer, ditto.
Wilſon and Croſs, ſoap houſe, croft head.
Wilſon Henry, maltman, town head.
Wilſon William, bleacher, gauze ſtreet new town.
Wood Francis, tobacconiſt, high ſtreet.
Wylie William, merchant, croſs.
Wilkie Peter, grocer, ſmith hills.
Wright Robert, tobacconiſt high ſtreet.
Wright Adam, copper ſmith high ſtreet.
Young John, Stamp maſter, moſs row.

A

A Iken Mifs Jean, merchant, laigh ftreet.
A Alfton Gavin and Co. ditto herring ftreet.
Alexander John, ditto new ftreet.
Anderfon, Fullerton, and Co. ditto cathcart ftr.

B

B Ain John, fhip mafter, laigh ftreet.
B Bain Alex. and Co. grocers, ditto.
Bartholomew James, flefher, flefh market ftreet.
Bartholomew John, ditto ditto.
Black Archibald, baker, new ftreet.
Black John, cooper, herring ftreet.
Black John, fhoe maker, laigh ftreet.
Boog Thomas, merchant, ditto.
Boyd William, fhip mafter, broad clofs.
Bow William, copper and white iron fmithlaigh ftr.
Boyle Mrs. vintner, ditto.
Brown Alex. wright, cathcart ftreet.
Brown Alex. upholfterer, ditto.
Brown William, fail maker, laigh ftreet.
Brownlee John and William, copper and white
iron fmiths, new ftreet.
Brown James and Co. painters, cathcart ftreet.
Brown John, fhip mafter, laigh ftreet.
Brown Donald, ditto ditto.
Brown Hugh and Co. falt coats rope work.
Buchanan Robert, meafurer of timber, cathcart
ftreet.
Buchanan John, fenior, merchant.
Buchenan John, Junior ditto.

C

CAmpbell and Cuthbert, merchants, laigh ftreet,

Campbell, Lee, and Co. Gourock rope work

Campbell John, ditto cathcart ftreet.

Campbell John, ditto ditto.

Campbell Duncan, ditto ditto.

Campbell Alex. late comptroller, ditto.

Campbell Pollock, comptroller of cuftoms, ditto.

Campbell Neil, aud Co. merchants, ditto.

Campbell Alex. land waiter, ditto.

Campbell John, grocer, ditto.

Campbell Patrick, writer, cathcart ftreet.

Campbell John, jeweller, long vennel.

Cameron Alex. vintner, laigh ftreet.

Caldwall William, cooper, long vennel.

Carmichael John. watch and clock maker, new ftreet.

Carfwell Robert, mafon, cathcart ftreet.

Cathcart John, merchant, laigh ftreet.

Carmalt John, ditto cathcart ftreet.

Chambers William, flefher, flefh market ftreet.

Clark William, hardware man, new ftreet.

Colquhoun, Campbell, and Co. merchants.

Colquhoun David, furgeon, cathcart ftreet.

Colquhoun John, wright and cabinet maker, broad clofs

Colquhoun James, agent, laigh ftreet.

Crawford James fenior, merchant, ditto.

Crawford Hugh fenior, meffenger ot arms, ditto.

Crawford Hugh junior, writer, ditto.

Crawford John fenior, cooper, herring ftreet.

Crawford John junior, ditto ditto.

Cunningham George, collector of cuftoms, laigh ftreet.

* * * * * * * * * * * * * * * * * *

D

DEas Mrs. milliner, new ſtreet.
     Donald William and Co. merchants, laigh ſtreet.

Douglaſs Duncan, ſhip maſter, cathcart ſtreet.
Drummond Alex baker, laigh ſtreet.
Duncan John, pilot, ditto.
Duncan James, ditto ditto.
Duncan Andrew, hatt maker, new ſtreet.

E

Ewing James and Co. merchants, laigh ſtreet.
Ewing Alex vintner, cathcart ſtreet.

* * * * * * * * * * * * * * * * *

F

FAirlie John, wright, cathcart ſtreet.
     Ferguſon Archibald, cooper, ditto.
Ferguſon John, ditto ditto.
Forſyth Mrs. bookſeller, laigh ſtreet.
Frazer James, land waiter, ditto.

G

GAlt William, baker, new ſtreet.
     Gemmil James, merchant, cathcart ſtreet.
Gemmil David, merchant, fleſh market ſtreet.
Glaſsford Matthew, ditto laigh ſtreet.
Gordon and Miller, ditto Cathcart ſtreet.

Graham John, copper and white iron fmith, laigh
 ftreet.
Graham William, ditto new ftreet.
Graham Hugh, accountant, cathcart ftreet.
Grindlay William, grocer, laigh ftreet.

* * * * * * * * * * * * * * * * *

H

HAmllton John and Co. merchants, herring
 ftreet.
Hamilton William and Co. ditto.
Hally James, grocer, new ftreet.
Hayman John and Co. ditto laigh ftreet.
Harvie James, fmith, ditto.
Herdman James and Co. merchants, long ven-
 nel.
Hendry Samuel, grocer, laigh ftreet.
Hill Robert, horfe fetter, flefh market ftreet.
Holmes John, grocer, cathcart ftreet.
Hopkins Mrs. vintner, new ftreet.
Humphry William, mechant. laigh ftreet.

J

JAmiefon and Matthie, merchants, laigh ftreet.
 Jamiefon Andrew, baker, ditto.
Jamiefon Malcom, grocer, new ftreet.
Johnfton John and Co. merchants, long vennal.
Johnfton Mrs. vintner, laigh ftreet.

K

KEnnedy James and Co. merchants, laigh. ſtreet.

Kennedy John, wright and block maker, cathcart ſtreet

Ker Duncan, ſhip maſter, long vennal.

Ker Archibald, grocer, laigh ſtreet.

Key William, taylor, new ſtreet.

Kippen John and Co. merchants, cathcart ſtreet.

King Robert, cooper, laigh ſtreet

Kilpatrick George, vintner, long vennal.

Kirkwood Hugh, maſon, ditto.

L

LAird John and Co. rope work, laigh ſtreet.
Laird Gabriel, bookſeller, ditto.

Lang William, merchant, ditto.

Lang James, grocer, cathcart ſtreet.

Lang James, junior, ditto. laigh ſtreet.

Lancaſter George, vintner, cathcart ſtreet.

Lamont Archibald, baker, ditto.

Leitch and Mitchell, merchants, laigh ſtreet.

Leitch John, ditto ditto.

Love James, ditto ditto.

Lyle James, bookſeller, ditto.

M

MAlcom, Ritchie, and Leitch, merchants, new ſtreet.

M'Alman, ſurgeon, ditto.

M'Alpin William, bookſeller, ditto.

M'Alpin Thomas, grocer, laigh ſtreet.

M'Aulay John, merchant, laigh ſtreet.

M'Aulay Aulay, ditto fleſh market ſtreet.

M'Auſlan John, merchant, laigh ſtreet.

M'Auſlan George, grocer, cathcart ſtreet.

M'Auſlan Archibald, cooper, laigh ſtreet.

M'Allum Archibald, merchant, long vennal.

M'Callum Dougald, ditto laigh ſtreet.

M'Arthur Alex. carpenter, ditto.

M'Arthur Peter, victualler, ditto.

M'Arthur Peter, cooper, ditto.

M'Allaſter, Fleming, and Co. merchants, cathcart ſtreet.

M'Allaſter William, officer of Exciſe, ditto.

M'Cunn Thomas, merchant.

M'Donald Alex. merchant, herring ſtreet.

M'Gibbon Daniel, ditto laigh ſtreet.

M'Gowan Daniel, ditto ditto.

M'Gowan Archibald, corn dealer, new ſtreet.

M'Farlane John, jeweller, ditto.

M'Farlane John, baker, cathcart ſtreet.

M'Fee Robert, grocer, new ſtreet.

M'Iver John, merchant, herring ſtreet.

M'Intoſh William, ditto cathcart ſtreet.

M'Kellar Patrick and John, ditto laigh ſtreet.

M'Kellar Daniel, ditto new ſtreet.

M'Kendrick Robert, grocer, broad clofs.

M'Larty Alex. ſhip maſter, cathcart ſtreet

M'Lauchlane Charles, grocer, laigh ſtreet.
M'Lauchlane Duncan, victualler, ditto.
M'Millan Archibald, baker, ditto.
Miller William, pilot, ditto.
Miller James, ditto ditto.
Miller John, baker, cathcart ſtreet.
Miller Thomas, furgeon, laigh ſtreet.
Mitchell Peter, merchant, ditto.
Morriſon William and Co. ditto cathcart ſtreet.
Morris Quintin, grocer, laigh ſtreet.
Morris Peter, wright, fleſh market ſtreet.
Moodie John, writer, broad clofs.
Moodie John, grocer, laigh ſtreet.
Muir James, vintner, ditto.
Munn Angus, merchant.

N

Neilſon William, merchant, laigh ſtreet.
Nimmo, druggiſt, ditto.
Noble James, ſhip maſter, cathcart ſtreet.

P

PAgan John, land waiter, laigh ſtreet.
Paterſon William, writer, ditto.
Park James, ſhoe maker, ditto.

R

RAmſay Andrew, merchant, laigh ſtreet.
Rankine John, ſupervifor of Excife, cathcart ſtreet.

Ritchie Duncan, barber, laigh ſtreet.
Ritchie Dougald, inn-keeper, ditto.
Roy John, ſmith, ditto.
Roſs David, merchant.

S

SCott James, merchant, long vennal.
Scott James, ſenior, grocer, laigh ſtreet.
Scott James, junior, ditto ditto.
Scott John, carpenter, ditto.
Scott Robert, ſhoe maker, fleſh market ſtreet
Scott John, fleſher, ditto.
Shaw James, ditto ditto.
Shaw Thomas, ſugar houſe.
Shearer James, victualler, laigh ſtreet.
Shaw Daniel, merchant, ditto,
Sinclair Robert and Alex. ditto cathcart ſtreet
Simpſon and M'Farlane, wrights and block makers
    cathcart ſtreet.
Smith William, grocer, ditto.
Smith Duncan, carpenter, laigh ſtreet.
Snodgraſs John, writer, cathcart ſtreet.
Stewart John, merchant, laigh ſtreet.
Stewart, Rodger, and Robert ditto cathcart ſtreet.

T

TAylor Malcom, grocer, laigh ſtreet.
Taylor Archibald, ſmith, ditto.
Thomſon Archibald, ſhip maſter, cathcart ſtreet.
Thomſon Archibald, grocer, laigh ſtreet.
Thomſon James, tobacconiſt, ditto.

Townfend Robert, watch and clock maker, cathcart ftreet.
Turner John, fmith, laigh ftreet.

❋❋❋❋❋❋❋❋❋❋❋❋❋❋❋

W

Walkingfhaw James, merchant, laigh ftreet.
Walker Peter, tobacconift, new ftreet.
Watfon James, merchant, cathcart ftreet.
Watfon Andrew, infurance brokes, new ftreet.
Watfon William, bookfeller, ditto.
Watfon John, baker, ditto.
Weir Archibald, grocer, laigh ftreet.
Wilfon John, fhip mafter, ditto.
Wilfon John, ditto cathcart ftreet.
Wilfon Archibald, merchant, ditto.
Wilfon Nathan, writer, laigh ftreet.
Wilfon John, grocer, ditto.
Wilfon John, teacher of Englifh, ditto.
Wilfon John, grocer, new ftreet.
Wood Gabriel, merchant, cathcart ftreet,
Wood Andrew, change keeper, laigh ftreet.
Wright Robert, fhip mafter, ditto.
Wylie David, watch and clock maker, ditto.
Yuile Mrs, bookfeller, ditto.

A LIST of the MERCHANTS, &c. of Port Glaſgow, 1783

A

ADam and Anderſon, maſons.
Aiken James, merchant.
Anderſon John, hammerman.

B

BAnnatyne John, merehant.
Barr Patrick, cooper.
Barr John, junior, watch and clock maker
Bell William and Co. merchants.
Beaton David, ſhoe maker.
Boyd John, ſhip maſter.
Brown, Robert, ſenior, ditto.
Brown Robert, junior, ditto.
Buchanan Peter, vintner.
Burrows Edward, collector of cuſtoms.

C

CArmichael James, Surgeon.
Campbell Colin, ſhip maſter.
Clark William, wright.
Clouſton John, ſhip maſter.
Crawford, Stevenſon, and Co. merchants.
Crawford, King, and Co. ſugar houſe.

Crawford John, ſhip maſter,
Cunningham, John merchant.
Cumming Robert and Son, ditto.
Cumming Daniel, merchant.

D

DOugal Patrick and Co. merchants,
    Douglas Robert, ſhip maſter.
Douglaſs Robert and Son, merchants.
Dunlop John, ditto.
Dunlop, King junior, and Co. rope work.
Dunnet John, ſhip maſter.

E

Edgar Thomas, merchant.
   Ewing John, ſhip maſter.
Ewing John, merchant.

F

FAirie James, ſhip maſter
   Ferrier William, grocer.
Fitchet Robert, baker.
Foſter Thomas, merchant.
Foſter John, ditto.
Foſter James, Surgeon.

Foulis Allan, senior, wright.
Foulis Allan, junior, ditto.
Fullerton John, ship master.

G

Gardner James, ship master.
Glasford James, cooper.
Gordon James, ship master.

H

Hay Francis, ship master.
Hunter James and Patrick, merchants.
Hunter Malcom, wright.

J

Jamieson Robert and Co. merchants.
Jamieson John, ship master.

K

Ker Edward, ship master.
Keith Alex. ditto.
Keir Thomas and Son, merchants.
King James, senior, ditto.
King James, junior, ditto.
King William, ditto.
King John, cooper.
Kirkland Richard, watch and clock maker.
Kinnier Wiillam ship master.
Kinnier Robert. ditto.

***

L

L Aird Alex. merchant.
, Laird David, wright.
Livingſton Charles, ſhip maſter.
Livingſton John, merchant.
Longmuir James, ſhip maſter.
Luſk John, ditto.
Lyon Andrew, watch and clock maker.

***

M

M 'Arthur Alex. bookſeller.
M'Dougald, John, ſhip maſter.
M'Farlane Duncan, ditto.
M'Farlane Graham, baker.
M'Gill Thomas, ſhip builder.
M'Gill William, ſhip maſter
M'George John and Son, agents.
M'Gie George, ſmith.
M'Kechnie Alex. ſhip builder.
M·Kellar John, merchant.
M'Lachlane Alex. and Co. ditto.
M'Mutrie Hugh, copper and white iron ſmith
M'Millan Alex. wright.
M'Millan Andrew, merchant.
Mackie William, ſhip maſter.
Marſhall Alex. baker.
Milliken, Hunter and Co. merchants.
Milliken Hugh and Co. ditto.
Miller William, ditto.
Molliſon Alex. ſurgeon.
Moore Benjamin, ſhip maſter,

Montgomery John, fhip mafter.
Morris Hugh, ditto.
Murdoch George, comptroller of cuftoms.

Noble James, fhip mafter.
Peacock Robert, merchant.

R

R Amfay, Howat, and Co. merchants.
Ritchie Duncan Hammerman.
Robertfon Benjamin, merchant.
Rowand Stephen, ditto.
Rofe John.

* * * * * * * * * * * * * * * * *

S

S Cott William, copper and white iron fmith.
Shaw James and Co. merchants.
Shearer William, grocer.
Smith and Howat. merchants.
Steel, Jamiefon, Lyon, and Co. ditto.
Steven Alex. grocer.
Stewart John, fhip mafter.
Tarbet John, fhip mafter
Troop Andrew, ditto.

* * * * * * * * * * * * * * * * * * *

W

W Atfon Alex. writer.
Weir Daniel, merchant.
Wilfon John, ditto.
Wilkie Thomas, fhip mafter.
Wood John and Co.